RAYDENCRAFFT

M. ALAN YATES

ILLUSTRATED BY

M. ALAN YATES

Visit the author at www.RAYDENCRAFFT.com

Library of Congress Cataloging-in-Publication Data

Yates, M. Alan
Raydencrafft / by M. Alan Yates
ISBN-13: 978-0-6151-4991-2 (paperback)
[1. Shape-shifters—Fiction. 2. Mutants—Fiction. 3. Telekinesis—Fiction. 4. Fire-starters—Fiction. 5. Fate—Fiction. 6. Friendship—Fiction. 7. Fantasy stories]
I. Title: At head of title: Raydencrafft. II. Title.

Printed in the United States of America

FOR:

My wife, Kathy,
for her patience, love and support.

My daughter, Sarah Jessica,
for her endless ideas.

My mother, Angie,
for her eagle eye.

ACKNOWLEDGMENTS

This book may not have ever been completed without the generous help of many people. This is especially the case with Debbie Herman. Without hesitation, she came to my aid as I progressed through the peaks and valleys of the writing process.

Furthermore, I am forever indebted to my wife, Kathy, for her good judgment in shaping the story. Thanks also to my daughter, Sarah, for her nonstop enthusiasm.

Kudos also go to Dimitris Kolyris at Popdog Fonts, for his wonderful Tom Violence font, and for the assistance he gave me. For other great fonts, please visit his website at: Popdog_fonts.tripod.com.

Thanks also to Gregfonts for their Nightsky font, Larabiefonts.com for their Interplanetary font, Utopia Fonts for their Dael Calligraphy font, Pizzadude.dk for their Asqualt font, and, lastly, GemFonts for their Old Copperfield font.

And very special thanks to my mother, Angie, and my wife, Kathy, for the thankless job they did in proofreading the manuscript.

The support and suggestions they all gave freely is deeply appreciated.

Contents

RAYDENCRAFFT

Prologue

Three hundred years ago, the last die had been cast. From what seemed the edge of eternity, *She* who desired all things was swept from the Emerald Mountains. At last, the hatred born from her boundless greed had washed away.

Across the valley, the mountains basked in the glow of the sun as it descended into the west. Far on the horizon, lightning tore the darkening sky—a forewarning of a distant thunderhead that lay to the north. As twilight fell, the crescent moon, high in the east, floated among an endless display of shooting stars. It was a wild sky that celebrated this fateful night with brilliant streaks and blinding flashes.

In a hail of stardust, the heavens threw a veil of light over the gathering that rallied at the base of Mount Crittendome. Gazing up the summit's craggy face, they stood awestruck in the aftermath of what had come to pass.

Standing above the fellowship, a tall, rugged man stared down at them from atop a crude rock platform. Fierce and resolute, he had green eyes that were deep, intense, and as fiery as the emerald torch which crowned the staff he held—his name was Damon Raydencrafft. "My friends, we have remained steadfast in our resolve. In the wake of our victory, her dark legions have fled to the underground. Soon, these mountains, our home, will see their past glory reborn." Glancing at the turbulent sky, he tempered his exhilaration and looked out over his company. "Today, we have prevailed, but not without the painful loss of those who gave their lives to defend our cause. We must never forget the price they paid, for we are the last of the Traymontayne, and all that remains of the Outlanders." Many in the gathering sobbed as others lowered their heads in tribute to family and friends who died by her hand.

As his expression grew somber, Damon raised his staff and gazed at its shimmering flame. "On this hallowed ground, we shall build a great house as testament to the sacrifice they made—a conservatory designed solely to preserve our culture and teach the elemental arts to the generations that follow. Within this haven, our kind can live without fear of being singled out. Free from persecution, they will learn to understand the need for tolerance and the ideals of discipline and control—in order to keep the past from repeating itself—"

PRESENT DAY...

As their SUV approached the gates of the railcar entrance to the Raydencrafft Conservatory, the young brother and sister in the back seat awoke from a restless slumber. With nervous anticipation, they eyed the iron gateway, and wondered what was in store for them—

Chapter One

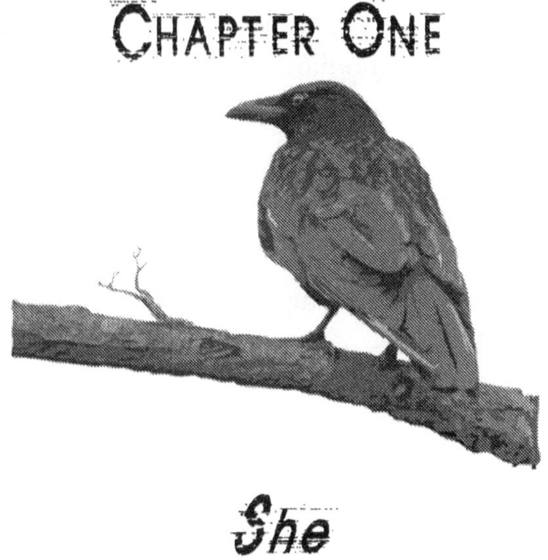

She

Two months earlier...

Paige gazed restlessly at the park through the rain streaked window. Only a misty drizzle remained as the sun peeked through the dark clouds. *At last, it stopped,* she thought. *Maybe now we can go outside and do something – anything.*

As her mind wandered, tiny beams of sunlight ebbed and flowed through the trees, seeping into the shadows. *Well, at least they've got a nice park. It's a whole lot better than this concrete parking lot they call a school.* Putting her nose to the glass, her emerald eyes widened. *Wait, is that somebody hiding in the bushes?* She squinted and quickly shook off the notion. *Oh, get a grip – shadowy stalkers in the bushes? Mom's right, maybe I have been watching too many scary movies.*

Shifting in her seat, she frowned at her brother, who looked almost as bored as she did. "Preston, how long do you think this will take?" she asked. Grabbing her copper hair, she tugged on it and moaned. "I just want to go home. My head's really pounding."

With a scowl, he stared at her and shrugged. "I don't know—not much longer, I hope." Glancing at his parents, and then toward the principal's office, he drew in a deep breath and sighed. At a hair over thirteen, he had a tall and lanky frame, and *oozed* sports from every muscle in his body. Along with a sprinkle of freckles dotting his face, he had a shiny new set of braces that kept him from showing the playful grin she'd long grown accustomed to. Like her, he bore a small birthmark on his neck in the shape of a crescent moon.

"I hate this," Paige said, rocking in her seat. "Why do we have to find a school so soon? We only moved a week ago, and we haven't even unpacked." Unhappily, she dropped her head, then gazed into his eyes which were each a different color—one green and the other blue. "Besides, you know I'm going to get picked on again. I just know it. The short girls always get the worst of it."

Running a quick hand through his sandy hair, Preston stared at her lightly freckled face, all eleven years of it, and slipped on his baseball cap. "Sis, come on, don't worry. I'll join the munchkin brigade and watch out for you, how's that?" he asked as she crossed her arms and sulked. "Anyway, I still think you're worrying about it way too much. Middle school isn't that bad—it's just a lunch break with a load of boring homework tossed in."

"Mr. and Mrs. Brandymire, I'm Principal Finnis," said the giraffe of a man as he offered his hand. Throwing Paige and Preston a dismissive smile, he turned his attention back to their parents. "Why don't we talk in the conference room?" he suggested, motioning to his secretary. "Ms. Burlley, show the children the Chatham Express while we go over their paperwork."

Handing them each a copy of the school newspaper, the mousy little woman beamed from ear to ear. "Principal Finnis always puts a lot of fun facts in each issue," she said, then waddled back to her desk.

"Boring," Preston whispered, frowning at the paper. Folding it into an airplane, he looked over his creation while Paige tried to finish reading her copy. Minutes later, she sighed and dropped it next to her.

"I can't finish it either," she said, fidgeting in her seat. "I hope Mom and Dad are almost done."

Closing an eye, he pumped the paper plane back and forth, contemplating its flight potential. *Hmmm, which is better – a great airplane or a boring newspaper? OH, NO!* Suddenly, the plane shot from his hand, and whizzed by Ms. Burlley on a collision course with Principal Finnis, who'd walked out from the conference room seconds before. Hours seemed to pass in the instant it took for the plane to smack him square in the forehead. Dumbfounded, the principal stood there frozen in place, turning five shades of red as he tried to speak. Stammering, he snatched up the airplane and unfolded it, then glared at them.

"Sorry about the...ummm, airplane...and your newspaper," Preston said glumly, "really."

Without uttering a word, Principal Finnis threw them a cruel grin as he slammed the door behind him.

Great. Welcome to your new school, Preston thought. *Just great.*

BEEP—BEEP—BEEP—BEEP! Preston flew out of bed as he

tried to punch the snooze button, but knocked the clock to the floor instead. Slowly, the jackhammer feeling in his brain subsided. *Crud, this can't be the first day of school. Please let this be a nightmare.*

Having a reputation for barely being able to communicate before ten in the morning, he grumbled as he tossed on some clothes, then stumbled into the bathroom and tried to get his hair to stay down. "Paige, where's my toothpaste? I told you to leave my stuff where I put it." Stomping in, she shook her head and threw open the medicine cabinet, pointing at the tube as she left. "Hey, you know I never put it in there."

Paige fit the picture of a complete neat freak, plain and simple. Unsurprisingly, she was his exact opposite, as he never had a problem slipping half-eaten pieces of pizza into his homework.

"Preston, we're late," Paige said, squirming at the front door. "You better hurry, Mom's already in the car."

Grabbing a breakfast bar, he scooped up his open backpack, and in a rush for the door, dumped it all over the floor. "Geez, I can't believe how this day's starting," he moaned. Quickly, Paige helped him shovel up the debris, then, together, they raced outside.

"Everything all right back there?" their mom asked as she turned into the school's driveway. Nodding like a couple of bobble-head dolls, they both jumped out. "Preston, try not to get into any trouble—don't talk in class, listen to your teachers and watch out for your sister."

Cocking his head to one side, he rolled his eyes and frowned. "Okay, Mom, I got it."

"And Paige, try to relax, everything will be fine," she said as Paige forced out a smile. "Well, be good. I love you both." With a wave, she drove away.

"Ummm, we better hurry," Preston said. As they weaved

through the crowd, the last bell rang, and like a gunshot signaling the start of a race, everyone sped up in a mad dash for the entrance.

Rapidly, a flood of kids rushed past them as Preston stopped and grabbed the side of his head. "Preston, what's wrong?" Paige asked. "You look as white as a ghost."

"I don't know," he mumbled, rubbing his temples, "I'm not feeling so good." Seeing the worry on her face, he took a deep breath and started toward the entrance again. Paige reached the doors first, then waited for him to catch up. Suddenly, a blazing orb of indigo plasma came barreling at her from the shadows in the park, spinning her around as it struck her full-force. Shocked silence gave way to chaos as the mass of kids scrambled, slamming her into the doors.

In an all out panic, Preston tried to push his way through to Paige, but the mob shoved him backwards to the pavement. Struggling to his feet, he grimaced as a razor-sharp pain shot through his right arm. Frantic, he dove into the fray as he watched the crowd trample her. "Paige! Get away from her! Get back!"

While he fought the rabble surrounding his sister, a woman clad in a hooded cloak approached him stealthily from across the street. Resembling an unformed clay doll in its fledgling stage of creation, *She* peered out from beneath her hood—her flaming indigo eyes transfixed on an unaware Preston.

"Get off of her!" he screamed, pulling at the crowd. "Paige!" Instantly, everything blurred. His head pounded to the beat of a mad drummer, worsening with each step *She* took in his direction. Covering his ears, he tried to quiet the roaring avalanche in his mind, when, unexpectedly, an eerie hush filled the air. Bit by bit, he cracked open an eye. Before him, a strange veil of emerald green washed over everyone as a pulsating wave of fiery light flowed from him. Plowing through the crowd, the surging energy pulse smashed into the entrance then reversed course, sending the hooded woman spiraling through the trees in the park.

Exhausted, Preston dropped to his knees, turning as *She* shrieked and thrashed wildly along her backward flight. As her mad screeching reached a mind numbing pitch, *She* burst into a shimmering murder of indigo crows. Filling the sky, the birds scattered, leaving silence in their wake.

Wheeling around, his heart jumped at the sight of his sister lying unconscious among the dazed students that littered the pavement. "Paige!" he shouted, running to her side. "Paige, come on, wake up." Quickly, he slipped his hands under her and tried to lift her, but gasped as the pain coursed through his arm again. "Somebody help! She needs help, please!"

Inside the entrance, a number of horrified teachers and students ran to the doors as the school nurse hurried over to them. Taking Paige's wrist in her hand, the nurse's thin, lined face went pale. "Stay with her while I find help, okay?" As a shudder ran down his spine, Preston stared at her and nodded.

Gingerly, he cradled his right arm, wincing as he looked down at Paige. "Open your eyes—please." Taking her hand, he began to regret every rotten thing he'd ever said or done to her. All at once, her crescent birthmark turned a beautiful emerald green as a sparkling wave of flames flowed from his hand and washed over her. Swirling inward, the fire vanished, taking her cuts and bruises with it.

Gawking at his glowing hand in disbelief, he gazed down at Paige, then back to his hand. Suddenly, she let out a faint groan as her eyes opened slowly and darted from Preston to the pavement in front of her.

"What…what happened?" she asked.

"Paige, you'd never believe me if I told you."

Chapter Two

Splash Damage

"One more week and I get this cruddy thing off," Preston said, shoving a pencil under his cast. Sitting across from him, Paige watched with growing curiosity. "It itches like crazy. If I could only just...get...get...ah, got it."

"Mom told you not to do that, remember?" she scolded. "Besides, you're going to have a bunch of pencil marks all over your arm when you get it off."

Actually, fracturing his arm had turned out to be a good thing, since he and Paige wound up in the emergency room long before a truckload of police showed up. In the days that followed, they faced a ton of questions, but, since neither of them had a clue of what really happened, no one could do much about it.

All the same, five weeks had come and gone, yet the lull had barely made a dent in stopping the nasty rumors that were sprouting like weeds, making life at school miserable.

"Preston, it's almost time for class," Paige said impatiently. Downing the last of his soda, he threw a half-eaten apple into his backpack as she rolled her eyes in disgust.

"You know, that's not a trashcan on your back," she said, pointing to his backpack as she carefully rewrapped her leftovers. "You're always wondering why your assignments are a gooey mess, just take a peek in there and you won't have to wonder anymore."

Sitting in the back row of algebra class, Preston tapped a pencil against his desk, thinking about anything but math. In fear of falling into a math-induced coma, he focused on the chalkboard, trying desperately to concentrate. Across the sea of seats, the ticking of the wall clock followed the monotonous droning of his teacher, who was scribbling something on the board that looked more like ancient hieroglyphics than math. "Okay, does anyone know what this equation is called?" he asked, pointing to the chicken scratch. "Raise your hands if—"

BRRR_RING! The last bell rang as the hands of the clock reached two-thirty. At that moment, it felt like someone had screamed the word *fire* as a stampede broke out, leaving the teacher standing there in mid-sentence.

Happy to escape the math morgue, Preston headed to Paige's last class. Turning the corner, he slowed to a crawl as he saw his sister at the other end of the hall. Surrounded by four girls, all but one an eighth-grader, Paige whimpered tearfully as they shoved her hard against the lockers, knocking her to the floor.

"Hey! Leave her alone!" Preston shouted as he ran toward

them. "Get away from her!"

The girls stared at him as he slid to a stop. Suddenly, he dropped to the floor and grabbed the side of his head as a curtain of emerald light fell over him.

No! Please, his mind raged, *not again!*

Instantly, the girls scattered, but before they could reach the exit, a pulsating orb of green fire came barreling at them. Wide-eyed, Paige sat petrified in the middle of the hallway as the mass of fiery plasma snowballed and swirled around her, leaving her untouched.

Seeing what pursued them, the girls ran screaming down the hall, bringing several teachers out from their classrooms. Without pause, the flaming sphere passed through them and hit the four girls like bowling pins, sending them sprawling across the floor. In seconds, a hush fell as everyone watched the girls struggle to their feet, looking as if they'd seen a ghost. Stunned, but unhurt, they gathered their scattered things and crept out the hall doors.

"Paige, we've gotta go before they figure out what happened," Preston whispered as he grabbed her backpack. Shaken, she stumbled as he pulled her through the exit. "I don't have time to explain right now, just keep moving."

On the walk home, he described every detail of their first day at school from the strangest to the most incredible, ending with what had just happened in the hall. "—and then that ball of whatever-it-was came out of nowhere—and you saw the rest." Searching Paige's face for a small hint of understanding, he choked on the horrified look she threw at him. Quickly, he tried to think of something to say to make things right, when to his surprise, she burst into tears and hugged him.

"I'm glad you're my brother," she said as he wiped her tears away. "I love you a lot."

"Ummm...uh—I love you too, just stop crying, okay?"

Finally, he felt a faint glimmer of hope. *Maybe all these things are happening for a reason,* he thought. *Only I'm not so sure what the reason is – yet.*

Chapter Three

Bottom of the Fourth

After earning a trip to the principal's office for the incident in the school hall, Preston laid low as the next week crawled by. At last, the day came for the unveiling of his new and improved right arm, marking the end of seven tedious weeks on his parent's disabled list.

"All right, Mister Brandymire, you wanted to tryout," Coach Newsome said as he grabbed some gear. "So, are you ready to show me what you've got?" Waving to a kid in the dugout, he waited for the boy to take his position on the pitcher's mound. "That's Joey, our backup pitcher. He'll toss you a few pitches and we'll see how things go."

Standing at home plate, Preston stared at the lanky string bean of a kid, and anxiously waited for the pitch. WOOSH! It flew past him faster than a speeding bullet. Turning back towards the pitcher, he looked at him with a little less confidence than before. *I don't get it. How can a scrawny kid like him throw like that? There's no way he's getting it past me again, not if I can help it.*

Preston readied himself and—WOOSH! Swinging at the next pitch, he missed, then spun around and wound up on his butt. Unbelievably, that pitch rocketed past him faster than the first, and even worse, Joey hadn't even broken a sweat. Grinning from under his blond buzz cut, the kid watched Preston from the mound, waiting as he tossed the ball into his glove.

With a scowl, Preston got up and dusted himself off. *Geez, I can't believe he's just a backup pitcher.* He held his bat out in front of him, lining it up on the boy's annoying smirk. Carefully, his eyes followed Joey as he came out of his wind-up and let another fastball fly. Swinging at it with all the concentration he could muster, Preston shot a rocket into left field—FOUL!

Come on, I had that one. I've got to hit the next pitch. I've got to—or I'm sunk. Wiping the sweat from his face, he glanced nervously at the coach, hoping beyond all hope for a miracle. Suddenly, Joey let loose a jaw dropping pitch that seemed to float on air. CRAACK! Preston's bat splintered into a thousand pieces as it met the ballistic missile Joey had thrown. Stumbling backwards, he gazed toward the outfield for a sign of the ball and found it rocketing over the center field fence. All around him, sparkling shards of wood lay scattered across the infield as he realized—*it* had happened again. *Oh, crud, I ask for help and I get this.* Shaking his head, he stared at the dugout, and found everyone gawking at the empty horizon.

Awkwardly, he stood there fidgeting as the pieces of his destroyed bat slowly lost their glint. "Wow…uh, it must have been a juiced ball or something—or maybe it got caught in the wind on the way up."

No matter how he tried to look at it, this green-glowing-whatever-it-was had worn out its welcome. Sure, it was kind of cool in a weird sort of way, but why did it have to be happening now? And what if it had something to do with that weird woman he'd sent screaming into the park? All of a sudden, an awful thought occurred to him. *What if I am a freak?* One thing he knew for sure, he'd better get a grip on things before he ran out of excuses and places to hide.

"Okay, you've made the team," Coach Newsome said, shaking his head as he handed Preston a uniform. "Practices are on Mondays and Thursdays at three, and we have the Centennial game next Wednesday at five."

Preston threw him an impish grin, deciding to press his luck a little further. "Coach? Do you think there's any way I might get a chance to play shortstop?"

Looking quite perplexed, the coach's eyes widened. "Short-stop?" he asked, scratching the side of his head. "Uh, let's see how well you do at practice first, and we'll talk about it afterwards, all right?"

The day of the city's centennial game at Lambert Field had finally come. Chatham was playing their cross town rival, Bancroft Middle School, a team they'd lost to far too many times to count.

On the drive there, Paige passed the time reading the street signs along the way, while Preston squirmed in the seat next to her. *Weird, look at all the birds. They're everywhere, even on the light poles,* she thought. *What are they – blackbirds? No, crows. Creepy.*

Pulling into the lot, they parked near Chatham's dugout and

piled out. Stretching, Preston glanced around, then shuddered as he gazed up at the trees. *What? Crows! No, She can't be back!*

"It looks like it might rain," his dad said, staring up at the birds. "They always act this way when the weather changes."

Pulling his sister aside, Preston put a finger to his lips. "Paige, do you remember what I told you about our first day at school?" he whispered as his eyes darted to the trees and then back to her. "About the crows I saw in the park."

Nervously, she peered at the birds and nodded. "I think *She's* here, I can feel it," he said as the crows cawed at one another. "Paige, watch out for yourself—and Mom and Dad too."

Standing deep in the outfield, Preston squinted at the trees again. The crows flapped about as they cackled back and forth, but no one seemed bothered by them at all. *I'm getting paranoid, they're just ordinary crows.* Glancing toward the clouds on the horizon, he shook his head. *Dad's right, it's probably going to rain.*

By the bottom of the fourth inning, it appeared as if Preston's overactive imagination had gotten the best of him. So far, everything had gone smoothly. Chatham had moved ahead of Bancroft five to three, and even better, he already had two hits under his belt. Stepping up to the plate, he got into his batting stance as the lights of Lambert Field magically came on.

Whoa! Stadium lights, he thought. *It's almost like being in the big leagues.*

From the stands, Paige watched Preston doggedly foul off one pitch after another. Dividing her time between his at-bat and the trees in the parking lot, she froze as a shiver ran through her. *The crows—where did they go?* Her eyes darted around the field and back to the trees. *What am I going to do?* Fearfully, she gazed down at Preston, hoping he noticed they'd gone, but as he hit a double into the outfield, her heart sank. *I've got to tell him.*

"Mom, I...ummm...I need to use the restroom," Paige said, giving her a weak smile. "I'll be right back." Hopping down from the bleachers, she walked quickly to the dugout, skirting along the back side of the stands. *It's too dark back here, I can't see anything.* She edged her way forward, stopping as she stared up the embankment leading to the railroad tracks behind the ballpark. *Wait – what's that? Somebody's on the tracks.*

Abruptly, the shadowy figure stopped and stood motionless as Paige tried to close the gap between them. *I hear something,* she thought as her eyes locked on a shimmering light approaching from the distance. *A train's coming! Oh my gosh, why is he still standing there?*

Terrified, her mouth fell open as the dark form hurled a wave of indigo flame at the freight train. An instant later, the wall of blue fire smashed into the forward cab, wrenching the locomotive from the tracks as the weight of its two cars thrust it toward the crowd. Spilling out a mad chorus of shrieks, the shape took to the air and hovered above the carnage as Paige stood in the path of the looming train.

From across the field, Preston ran past his panicked teammates. All around him chaos ensued as people scattered in every direction. Desperately, he tried to find his family when he saw what couldn't be possible.

"Paige!" he screamed. *Why isn't she trying to run? What's she doing?* "Paige!" Horror-struck, his eyes followed the wreckage as it tumbled down the embankment. All of a sudden, an emerald fountain of sparkling plasma sprang from Paige a second before the wall of steel swallowed her whole. Washing over the train at a break-neck speed, the rippling wave smothered the indigo inferno, transforming the wreck into a ghostly version of itself. Effortlessly, it passed through Paige like a phantom, and continued on through the stands and the crowd, leaving everything and everyone untouched. Finally, the train came to rest near the left field fence, its glow fading as it returned to solid form.

Am I dead? I must be, Paige thought as she peeked out from between her fingers, *but I don't feel dead.* With a dizzying buzz running through her head, she stumbled as Preston ran up to her.

"Paige! Are you okay?"

"Uh-huh, I'm all right—at least, I think I am, but I'm not sure what just happened. I almost—" she said as her eyes widened in fear. "PRESTON!" Following her line of sight, he looked up the rise, only to find a grotesque, luminous visage of a woman glaring down at them.

"*She* did this!" Paige screamed, pointing a trembling finger at her. "Why? What do you want?" Curiously, the woman stared at her, then focused her indigo gaze on Preston. Extending her grisly hand, *She* let loose a hail of blue orbs, trapping him in a fiery net as he dropped to his knees in agony.

"Preston!" Paige cried out, wrapping her arms around him. "Leave him alone! He didn't do anything to you!"

Seemingly unconcerned, *She* moved her index finger from side to side and peered coldly at Paige. "Why won't you leave us alone?" Paige shouted as several people came to their aid. Whipping around, the woman hit the unsuspecting crowd with a blast of kinetic energy, propelling them backwards onto the field. Dropping her guard for a split second, *She* loosened her grip on the blazing trap that surrounded Preston. Instantly, the net turned dark green as a whirling mass of blazing orbs shot from Preston and Paige, and roared toward the woman as *She* tried to escape. As the trap of her own making ensnared her, *She* struggled to free herself, letting out an ear-piercing shriek as *She* transformed into a swarm of indigo wasps. Swiftly, the cloud of buzzing insects retreated into the night, leaving everyone gazing at the horizon.

Bewildered, Paige stared wide-eyed at Preston as she pulled him to his feet. "Preston, your game," she said, sobbing as the sparkle of her birthmark washed away. "You didn't even get to finish it."

Preston ran a hand through his hair and gave her a feeble smile. "After all this, you're worried about a stupid baseball game—forget about it. But hey, you've got to admit, that sure was one amazing fourth inning."

Chapter Four

A Not so Fond Farewell

It had been five days since the disastrous Centennial game, and for the most part, everyone either considered Paige and Preston heroes or fiends of some sort. Even now, the debate raged on as the press and police clamored for first hand, blow by blow, accounts of the accident. But, no matter how much they wanted to forget that night, they couldn't ignore the fact that a freight train still sat smack dab in the middle of Lambert Field. And, since the wreck hit nothing on its way there, it became all too clear that something bizarre had happened.

As much as Paige and Preston hated to admit it, life at school had gotten even more unbearable now that their so-called freakish abilities went public. And, as if things couldn't get any worse, they'd even overheard their parents arguing about how *normal* they actually were.

"Things weren't so good today, were they?" Preston asked Paige as they headed out of school. From the look on her face, he already knew the answer. Shaking her head no, she stared at the ground as he put his hand on her shoulder.

"When I left my third period class today, someone tripped me, I think on purpose," she said tearfully. "All my books and things were scattered everywhere, and no one would even stop to help. They just stepped around me like I deserved it."

As she wiped her tears away, Preston skirted around the front of her, backpedaling as he walked. "Paige, things'll get better, I'm sure of it—you know why?"

"No—why?"

"Because things can't get much worse, can they?" he asked as she cracked a smile.

Pausing outside the gates of the ball field, he watched as his team warmed up, then turned to leave. "Preston, what about practice?" Paige asked. "Aren't you going?"

"No, I don't think so. Things haven't been so good with some of the guys lately," he said, glancing back toward the field. "Besides, I just want to get out of here."

Walking home in silence, they turned the corner to their block, when an odd little leprechaun of a man peeked out from behind a trashcan. "Excuse me, I'm kinda lost. Can ya help me?" he asked with a twinkle in his eye. "Oh, wait, I'm sorry—how rude of me, my name's Natewick Beadle." Putting a hand to her mouth, Paige giggled at him as he raised a bushy white eyebrow at her. "Oh, and what's so humorous, missy?"

"Ummm...ah, nothing really" she said, blushing.

Preston smirked at her, then stared curiously at Mr. Beadle. "So, what were you looking for?"

"Well, this may sound a bit odd, but an acquaintance of mine said he'd seen the strangest thing—said I should see it too before it goes," he said, pushing his half moon spectacles to the top of his nose. "Seems there's a train, of all things, resting in a field...ummm, Landirt or Lanssert Field, have ya heard of it?"

Paige eyed Preston nervously, then frowned at Mr. Beadle. "You mean Lambert Field?"

He smiled as if she'd hit the right note. "That's exactly right, *Lammert* Field," he said. "So, ya have heard of it."

Instantly, a cloud of gloom fell over Paige. "Yes, I...we've heard of it, but I'm not sure how to get there from here. Preston, do you know?"

"I think it's that way, but I've only been there once," he said, pulling his cap down around his eyes. "So, I can't help you much either. Uh, why do you want to go there?"

"Ummm, it's a wee bit complicated to explain ya see, but in a nut's shell, my acquaintance said some of the strangest things went on down there," he explained, tapping a finger against his chin. "So, I'm here to see for myself." Carefully, he studied their faces as he changed the direction of his question. "Oh, ya two wouldn't happen to know what went on, would ya?"

Tongue-tied, Preston gave Paige a blank stare as she nudged him in the side. "Uh, there's not much to tell," she said, sidestepping the question. "I mean, no one got hurt."

Mr. Beadle gazed quizzically at Paige, and then raised a brow at Preston. "Nothing at all? Hmmm, ya sure? I heard a woman sent the train flying from the rails. This wasn't true?"

With a shrug, Preston tried to hide the fact that he knew more than he wanted to let on. "Uh, Mr. Beadle, we've gotta get going, but I sure hope you find what you're looking for."

"Thank ya, it was nice talking to ya both." Smiling, he handed them each a small, smooth green stone that gleamed as it touched the palms of their hands. "A tad trinket for your time—they're blooms, a Laurelean Bloom to be precise. I've always loved their sparkling beauty."

"Laurelean Bloom? It's really pretty," Paige said, then gasped. "Oh my gosh, it's getting warm, but how? And what makes them glow like this?"

"Why, ya do, missy," he chuckled, "ya make them glimmer and glow."

Eyeing the stone, Preston frowned. "Mr. Beadle, I'm sorry, but we shouldn't take them," he said, making a face at Paige as she held hers tight. "I mean, they're nice and all, but we didn't do anything to deserve them."

"Oh, I won't hear of it. Besides, I've got a few too many as it is," he said, grinning. "Uh, but before I go, I gather your name is Preston, but I didn't get your name, missy."

"It's Paige," she said, smiling.

"What a pretty name it is. Paige—it rolls off the tongue. A pretty name for a very pretty lassie," he said as she blushed once again. "Well, I suppose ya need to get home—ya both take care now."

After taking only a few steps, Preston stopped and turned in the little man's direction. "Mr. Beadle, I just remembered, I…huh?" he said as his eyes darted down the sidewalk. "Hey, where'd he go?" Quickly, he ran up to the corner, but the odd little leprechaun had vanished.

"Expelled? They can't do that!" Preston shouted as his parents looked on in utter confusion. Breaking into tears, Paige ran into her bedroom as he sat there staring numbly at the wall. "So just like that, that's great," he said, shaking his head. "Why? We didn't do anything wrong." Pacing the room, he pulled at his hair as he tried to make sense of what was happening. *I don't get it. How can they be so wrong about us when we don't even know what's going on?* "Whatever," he said, tossing his backpack aside. "It's not like I'm going to miss that rotten school or its cruddy student body."

"Paige—Preston—let's get going," their mom yelled, grabbing her keys. "Now!"

Hastily, they rushed out the door, all but smashing into one another as they climbed into their SUV. Grinning from ear to ear, Preston slid across the seat and gazed out the window. *Great, so we're going back to Chatham where the fun never stops.*

"I don't know why you're so happy about going back there," Paige said as she scowled at him. "It makes me nervous."

"Sis, relax. All Mom has to do is pick something up from Principal *Unfriendly,* and we'll be in and out before you know it, you'll see," he said, smirking at her. "Besides, what can happen in just a couple of minutes?"

"Ah, Mrs. Brandymire, it's nice to see you again," Principal Finnis said in a sugary sweet tone. With a thin smile, he glanced at Paige and Preston. "Oh—and you too." Rolling their eyes, they sat down by the window as he snapped his fingers at his secretary. "Ms.

Burlley, would you get me the packet I put together for her." After searching her desktop, she stared timidly at him as the vein on the side of his neck began to bulge. "Ms. Burlley? The packet of school brochures—the one I told you to hold."

"Uh...ummm, I can't find it," she said, looking truly distressed. "I put it right here, but now it's gone."

"What? I asked you to do a simple thing and you still managed to botch it up," he shouted as he rifled through her desk. "Mrs. Brandymire, I apologize. If you'll give me a moment, I'll try to put another packet together for you." Pointing a bony finger at his secretary, he sneered at her. "We'll talk about this later."

"Geez, this is taking a lot longer than I thought," Preston said as Paige fiddled with the CD case she'd brought. Getting up from his chair, he stretched and grinned at her. "I'm going outside, you wanna come?" With a nod, she gathered up the loose CDs and followed Preston toward the exit. Suddenly, the lunch bell rang overhead. Hurrying to keep up, Paige bobbled the case, spilling its contents all over the floor.

"Preston! My CDs!" she screamed as the discs rolled across the room. "Help me!" Trying frantically to scoop them up, they bobbed and weaved through a flood of lunch-bound students, hitting the brakes as Principal Finnis walked out from his office.

"What in the—" he barked. Stepping out onto a *minefield* of shiny discs, his feet instantly slid out from under him. CRASH! BAM! A cloud of paperwork confetti rained down on him as he lay spread-eagle on the floor, gazing silently at the ceiling.

"Uh, are you all right?" Ms. Burlley asked awkwardly.

Sitting up, he glared at her, then turned his full attention to

Paige and Preston, who were standing there with CDs in hand. "Do I look all right?" he yelled as his secretary squirmed in place. "Well, do I?" Surrounded by a litter of school pamphlets, he struggled to his feet and glowered at their mother. "If you still want the brochures, I'll have them mailed to you," he said dismissively, "but right now, I'd much rather you leave."

"Paige! Preston! Get in the house—now!" their mom said. Slamming the car door, she shook her head as she left them standing there gawking at each other.

I don't get it, Preston thought. *Why is she mad at me? I didn't do anything—at least, not this time.* Tiptoeing inside, he grabbed the mail and sifted through it. In the middle of the stack, a strange envelope caught his eye. *Hey, it's addressed to me and Paige. Who'd send us something?*

"Hmmm, fancy," he whispered. "I bet it cost a lot." Made of green parchment paper, it had a sparkling dark green seal with a large letter 'R' in its center. Breaking the seal, he pulled out a light green piece of stationary.

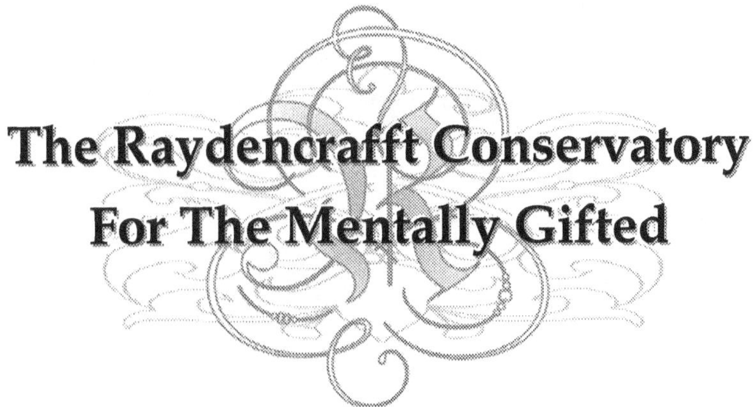

Chancellor Mathias Manderlane, O.C.M.

Dear Applicant(s):

It is our sincere pleasure to invite you to a pre-orientation at the Raydencrafft Conservatory, on the 17th of December at 3 pm. If you would like to attend, please contact our message service for further information at (888)-555-4967, ext. 537.

Since our first semester is already in progress, all who are accepted into our program will be required to enroll as soon as possible.

Many financial aid packages are available for new enrollees, such as academic scholarships, grants, etc. Pre-qualification is required.

In closing, we look forward to hearing from you, and hope that you will find our curriculum satisfying.

Warmest regards,

Mathias Manderlane

Mathias Manderlane, O.C.M.
Chancellor
South Emerald Way
Mt. Crittendome, Washington 99999

Mentally Gifted? Gimme a break. Maybe Paige – but me? No way. Setting the invitation down, he grinned. "Yeah, I've gotta show this to Mom. She'll never believe it—not in a million years."

Chapter Five

An Unexpected Reunion

As their SUV approached the gates of the railcar entrance to the Raydencrafft Conservatory, Preston rubbed the sleep from his eyes and squinted out the rain soaked window. "Paige," he said, nudging her, "we're here."

She shook herself awake and scowled at him. "Uh, but where'd they put the school?" Staring through the windshield toward the ivy-covered gateway, she wrinkled her nose at her mom as she leaned over the front seat. "There's nothing here—just mountains and trees—and nothing else."

Slipping on his baseball cap, Preston jumped out of the backseat and surveyed the area. "It must be through those gates, but if you ask me, this is a pretty creepy spot for a school."

"I thought this was an open house," Paige said. "Are we the

only ones here?"

"Yeah, it sure seems that way," he said, glancing up at the dark canopy of trees. "Uh, I don't know about this."

All around them, the ancient moss-grown hemlocks stood guard over the clearing like huge sentinels, deliberately concealing the entrance from unwelcome visitors. "Wow, they weren't joking, this place really is off the beaten path," their mom said as she looked around. "I can't imagine anyone finding it without directions."

"Off the beaten path? Mom, come on, this is more like an episode of *extreme* hiking," Preston said with a grin. "Heck, I'd leave a trail of bread crumbs to find our way back if I knew the wild animals wouldn't follow them and eat us."

"Wild animals? Preston, you're kidding, aren't you?" Paige asked as her eyes darted around the clearing.

He flexed his muscles and smirked at her. "Sis, don't worry, I'll protect you," he said, parading around like a big game hunter. Scoffing at his sarcasm, his mom walked towards the gated entrance, and eyed the eight symbols running along its outer border.

Quickly, Preston gave up the *hunt* and walked over to his mom, then peered through the gates into the tunnel beyond. "Whoa! It's pretty dark in there. Ummm, I don't think anyone's here," he said, pushing his face right up to the bars. "Hey, HELLO—anybody in there?"

Annoyed, his mom threw him a sharp glare. "Preston, if you think that's the way to make a good first impression, you're dead wrong," she quipped, pulling a note from her pocket. Unfolding the paper, she looked it over, then studied the doorway. "Okay, these symbols, this says we have to touch them in a certain order."

Placing her hand against the sun-shaped pictogram, she jumped back as it began to glow a brilliant yellow-orange. With uncertainty, she continued to press the icons in the correct order as they watched each one explode into a vibrant color of its own.

"Mom, can I try?" Paige asked eagerly.

"Sure, go ahead—that's the last one," she said, pointing to the crescent moon.

Paige held her breath as she touched the symbol and waited, but nothing happened, not even a spark. "Hey, what...why?" she said, staring dejectedly at her mom. "That's not fair, it didn't—" In mid-sentence, her mouth fell open as every symbol burst into brilliant emerald green flames. Taken by surprise, they all backed away as the iron gates groaned and flew open.

Inching their way inside, they peered into the darkness. A few feet up ahead, an unlit lantern hung from the ceiling. Almost falling head-first, Preston slowly moved towards it, when, mysteriously, the lamp lit on its own. "Uh, don't look at me, I didn't do it," he said as Paige made a face at him. "At least, I don't think I did."

"Maybe it's on automatic or something," Paige said, wrinkling her nose at it, "but green fire, that's kind of weird, don't you think?" Smirking, Preston took a few steps forward, then stopped as another lamp lit by itself.

"Hello. Oh, hello," a boisterous voice called out. "Is anyone there?"

"Yes...yes, we're here," their mom shouted as a giant of a man appeared from around the bend. Clad in a forest-green uniform, he had a bushy red moustache that sprouted from under his enormous nose and a smile that gleamed as bright as his ice blue eyes.

"I'm so sorry I'm late. I normally keep a tight schedule, but I had some mechanical problems which took a bit of time ta fix. I hope ya weren't waiting around too long," he said, stroking his moustache. "Oh, but where's my head? Silastar Ledbothom's my name, but ya can call me Silas for short. And let me guess, ya must be the Brandymires."

"Yes, we are—this is my son Preston and my daughter Paige, and I'm Bryce."

"Well, it's nice ta meet ya, one and all of ya," he said, grinning as he shook their hands.

One by one, Paige followed the platinum buttons of his uniform up to the shiny snowflake insignia on his collar. Biting her lip, she tugged at his jacket cuff. "Mr. Ledbothom, are you a train conductor? I think I saw a uniform like yours in a movie we rented."

Giving her a crooked smirk, he knelt down in front of her. "Firstly, I insist ya call me Silas, I'll have none of that *mister* stuff here. And secondly, your close, but sadly I'd need a *real* train for something like that." Getting up, he pointed to the passageway behind him. "Down yonder are the railcars, it's my post ta run them about halfway up the peak," he said, motioning with his hands as he spoke. "From there we'll move on ta the skycars and take them the rest of the way ta Crittendome."

"Skycars? Now, I've got to see this," Preston said as Paige stared uneasily at her mom and then Silas.

"Oh, don't ya worry, little lady. It's a lot of fun, and no one's ever gotten hurt whilst I've been on post," he said, pausing to think. "Well, there was that one time—ah, but that's another story." Pulling out his pocket watch, he glanced at it and waved them on. "Alas, we'd better be going or we'll be late, and we'd not want that now, would we? So, follow me."

Whistling as he led them through the twisting tunnels, the big man turned to them as the hum of machinery drowned him out. "Here we are—the railcar dock," he said, looking rather proud.

Bathed in the emerald light of several flickering lanterns, the dock had two sets of small tracks, each with its own engine and rail-cars resting on it.

Geez, they look like cars from a coal-mine, Preston thought. *I bet they're just as uncomfortable.*

"Okay, where would ya like ta sit?" Silas asked, putting on his gloves and goggles. "It's the off season, so ya have your pick of the litter."

"I've got dibs on the last car," Preston announced as they all climbed in. "Now, this is way better than I expected." After a sudden jerk, the cars lumbered forward as the engine pulled them deep into the mountain, clicking and clacking along the way. Here and there, the eerie green flame from a solitary lantern lit the passage as they journeyed through the winding maze.

Daylight began to filter into the tunnel from far ahead as the railcars moved up the rise, then gradually leveled off, grinding and screeching to a stop. "Ladies'n Gents, first stop—Mountaintop Sky-dock." The enormous dock housed two sets of railcar tracks and a massive cable turntable with a line of glass gondolas suspended from it. "Ya all should see the splendid view, just watch your step near the railing," the big man said as he gestured to the open end of the dock.

"Mom! Preston! Look!" Paige exclaimed, pointing past the guardrail. "It's so beautiful."

No longer hidden by the clouds, the sun shined in all its glory, reflecting off the mountaintops that broke through the mist. "Ah yes, the Emerald Mountains—truly a sight for my sore eyes," Silas said, flashing a wide grin. "Makes me glad ta have this here post."

Frowning, Paige tugged at his jacket. "Silas? I heard about these mountains in class—aren't they called the Cascades?"

Silas tapped a finger against his chin as he twisted his moustache in thought. "Why, ya are a smart little lady, aren't ya?" he said as she smiled proudly. "Ya're exactly correct, of course. Indeedy, the Cascades they are—I'm kinda fond of calling them by the name they were given when Mister Raydencrafft graced this here place way back when, but that's another story."

Walking up to the skycars, he flipped some switches, and the machinery came to life, humming and clinking as it got up to full speed. "One more stop ta go, and in a jiffy, ya'll be on your way." Steadying a gondola, he winked. "Just step right in and find yourself a comfortable spot, and I'll do the driving."

Effortlessly, Silas floated the skycar out over the mountains on its way toward Mount Crittendome. "Yes, Crittendome's the very heart of this here place. For centuries, it's been witness ta truly amazing things," he said, pointing eagerly at the horizon. "Ah, and there it is, the sparkling jewel on Crittendome's crown—Raydencrafft!"

Far below them, hundreds of brick and stone buildings, both modern and old-colonial, spread out across the valley like a small city. From up high, the campus resembled a stately east coast university, and for a brief moment, it felt as if they'd traveled back to the distant past.

"Silas? Those fields, what are they for?" Preston asked as he pointed down to a set of back-to-back diamond-shaped playing fields.

"Oh, them, that's where we play Pryttonn," he said as another thought jumped into his head. "It's sorta like baseball and sorta not, but I've never been much good at it myself—slow footed, I guess."

"Pryttonn?" Preston sputtered as he kept his eyes glued on the fields. "They look strange. How's it played?"

"Well, Mr. Preston, wish I could tell ya now, but Crittendome's looming ahead of us," he said resignedly. "It'd be my pleasure ta discuss the splendid points of Pryttonn on your trip back, how's that?"

With a reluctant nod, Preston scowled as their skycar floated into the dock. "Last stop—Crittendome Skydock," Silas said as he slid open the door. "Regrettably, we must part ways, but we'll certainly see each other a wee bit later, won't we?" Guiding them to a set of open-air glass elevators, he chose the nearest one, and waited as they climbed in. "Okay, just so ya know, ya all will take this here lift down ta the conservatory and someone will meet ya there."

As the elevator made its descent, the three of them stared through the glass, watching as streams of whitewater rushed down the mountainside. Below, a river snaked its way under a crossing bridge and around the base of an enormous stone hall.

Piling out, Paige and Preston ran onto the bridge, gazing up at the chiseled words that ran across the hall's face. "Manderlane?" Preston asked. "Who's that?"

Paige shrugged as she peered up at the wooden entry doors that shared the halves of a huge carved R. "Oh my gosh, they're humongous."

All of a sudden, the doors swung wide open, and out walked a sharply dressed white-haired little man. "Ah, Preston and Paige," he said with a playful wink. "It's nice to see ya again."

In one fell swoop, their mouths dropped open as they gawked at each other in shock. "Mr. Beadle?" they shouted. "But how?"

Chapter Six

The Secret Benefactor

"Preston! Paige! Wait just a minute, you know this man?" their mom asked as they stared blankly at her. "Perfect—I guess I'm the only one in the dark here. All right, I'll bite then, who are you and how do you know my children?"

"Ummm, it's quite a tale, but in a nut's shell, I'm Natewick Beadle, the Head Counsel of Admissions. As for our meeting, it took place a few days ago. I was kinda lost, and by a simple stroke of luck, they happened to help me find my way."

Throwing a stern look at Preston and then Paige, she took a deep breath. "So this is a coincidence," she asked, shaking her head, "a chance meeting and now this? I'm sorry, but I'm having trouble believing this."

"Mrs. Brandymire, I understand why ya might feel that way.

To be honest, I've never been one for happenstance myself," he said, twisting an eyebrow, "but with happenings as they were—ya know, the train wreck and all, we had to take great measures to stifle the mounting fervor surrounding your children. Fortunately, our influence stretches far beyond the boundaries of the conservatory in matters such as these."

Mr. Beadle gestured towards the hall and gave her a sympathetic smile. "I realize this is a tad much to swallow at one sitting, but how about this? Why don't I acquaint ya with the conservatory, and afterwards, ya and Chancellor Manderlane can talk. I promise ya, he'll be happy to respond to all your inquiries." He motioned for them to follow as he sprang up the steps leading to the entrance.

Yeah, right, there's no way he'll be able to open those doors, Preston thought, staring up at them, *not unless he has an army hidden somewhere.* But as Mr. Beadle waved his hand across them, they flew open on their own. Preston's eyes darted from the doors to the little man. *What—huh? How did he do that?* Grudgingly, he followed him inside, only to stop dead in his tracks seconds later. "Whoa! Do you see this? Indoor waterfalls! Boy, the closest we ever got to this was when the restrooms backed up at school."

Paige giggled at Preston as she gazed up at the large, circular light fixtures that hung from the ceiling. Giving off a strange hum, the shimmering glass spheres swirled from within as they lit the lobby. "Mr. Beadle?" she asked. "Those globes, I think there's something moving around in them."

"Oh, don't ya worry, they're just Dusken Glowflies—they're housebroken," he said, leaning in close to her ear, "and missy, I'd be pleased if ya called me Natewick." With another flick of his wrist, he effortlessly opened the rear doors, and stopped outside. "So, next on the list are the libraries—follow me, if ya please."

Walking down the steps, Preston lagged behind, waiting for them to move farther up the path. Quickly, he hopped back up the stairs. *There's a trick to making these doors open, I know it,* he thought, fanning his hand over them. *Huh? That should've worked—what a rip-off.* Shaking his head, he scowled at the doors, then ran to catch up with the others.

"So, ya couldn't figure them out, eh?" Natewick asked as Preston stared narrowly at him. "Well, don't let it get ya down, laddie. It took me way more than a few tries when I was a wee lad."

As they passed by the garden at the Main Library, Paige stopped and looked out over the lush green field of clover. In its heart stood a marble sculpture of a cloaked man holding a staff atop a rock pedestal. Fixing her eyes on the statue, she went pale, almost stumbling as she turned away. "Missy? Is there something wrong?" Natewick asked as Preston peered at her from over the little man's shoulder. "Ya don't seem at all yourself."

"No, I'm a little tired I think," she said, glancing at the marble figure again. "Natewick, that statue—who is it?"

"Ah, why that's Damon Raydencrafft, the conservatory's founder—a most important man for sure," he said somberly. "It's a shame he never saw the conservatory open, a true shame indeed. Well, we'd better go if we want to stay on schedule."

Journeying beyond the library's columned entrance, they soon discovered a treasure trove of all things past and present. While Paige examined one display case after another, Preston roamed through the ceiling-high bookshelves, scrutinizing the strange selection of books. Pulling a leather-bound volume off a shelf, he shook his head. *Spirit Manifestation And Its Effects On Mediumistic Phenomena? Huh? And I thought my last algebra book had a confusing title.* Quickly, he shrugged it off, and weaved his way back toward the entrance. Cutting between the stacks, he zigged when he should have zagged and plowed right into a little sprite of a man, knocking him to the floor.

"Hooligan! Oaf! Where did you learn your manners—in a back alley?" the man shouted as Preston gawked at him. "What? Cat got your tongue?"

Boy, if the plaster gnome in our neighbor's front yard ever gets lost, this little guy would fit right in, Preston mused. *Nah, he'd probably scare everybody away – and kill their grass.*

With a scowl, the tiny gnome slipped his hat back onto his hairless head, and stroked his white moustache and goatee. Sizing Preston up, he rubbed the leaf-shaped mark on his neck and sneered. "Boy! I demand an apology," he said, tugging his purple smock down over his enormous belly. "Well?"

Bent on pressing the issue, he locked his eyes on Preston, when, from out of nowhere, Natewick stepped between them. "Ah, Precept Grievley, is there a problem?"

"Oh, Head Counsel Beadle. Uh, yes—this boy came running carelessly down the aisle and knocked me down."

"Now, Ezra, it was most likely a simple mishap. Isn't that correct, Preston?" he asked tactfully.

"Yeah," Preston muttered, staring dismally at the precept. "Sorry."

"All right then, we need to move along."

Precept Grievley's face turned beet red. "You mean you're not going to do anything about this!"

Raising a brow, Natewick looked the precept in the eye. "No, the boy apologized, that should suffice for now. But, not to be rude, I should introduce ya to each other."

"Preston, this is Precept Grievley, the instructor for Earth Sciences and Green Leaf Studies for your class level. Now, as for Preston, he's our guest for the time being," he explained, "and, if ya hadn't noticed—" Bending down, he whispered into the precept's ear. "—he's a crescent."

Carefully studying Preston's birthmark, the precept's expression went blank. "I've never—how is that possible?" he mumbled. "Uh, I have to go." Grabbing his things, he scurried down the aisle, chattering as he went. "Young man, you simply ought to be more careful next time, this is not the place to play games."

Preston wrinkled his nose at him and took a deep breath. *I don't know, there sure are some really strange people at this school.* Before today, he'd never even heard of a precept, whatever that was. *And what's a green leaf?* Anyway, it still didn't explain why that little bald yard decoration took off so fast. *Great, now all I have to worry about are green leafs, gnomes and precepts – oh, boy.*

Their next stop was the student lodgings. Over the entrance, the words *Girl's Quarters, Levels 6th 7th 8th* were carved. Around the doorway, tile versions of the symbols they'd seen earlier at the railcar entrance were set in stone.

"Oh, don't tell me we have to press these to get in," Preston said with a frown. "Cuz, if we do, I'll probably wind up sleeping outside most of the time."

Testing her brother's hunch, Paige put her hand against a tile as Natewick walked up beside her and grinned. "Missy, don't ya listen to him. For this one, ya just have to use your hands."

Inside, they peeked into an empty sleeping chamber and gazed around the room. On each side sat an upper and lower bunk, and on the far wall, a large computer hutch. A beautiful mural showing the sky from day to night covered the ceiling, while images of waterfalls, mountains, and forest greenery decorated the sandstone walls.

After exploring the Museums of Art, Natural History, and Physical and Esoteric Sciences, they moved on to the theater complex. Happy to leave the snorefest behind, Preston shook himself awake as he pushed and prodded Paige out the exit. Once they were at the complex, he perked up as he ran towards the entrance. "Wow, movie theaters at school," he shouted gleefully, "now *that* kind of homework I can handle."

With the tour almost over, Natewick led them to the instructional halls. Walking up the steps, they drew the unexpected attention of a number of students who watched them from the large arched windows. Next to the entrance hung a sterling silver plaque which read, *Hall-A Wickvane Instructional Hall, generously donated by M.A. Wickvane, O.S.S. September 1802.* "Allrighty, we should stay as quiet as field mice since lessons are still going on," the little man whispered, "but, please feel at ease to look through the glass if ya like."

Wandering along the long hall of classrooms, they peered into a large auditorium packed with students all dressed in dark forest-green school uniforms. One by one, Preston studied each face, when, out of the blue, one caught him—hook, line, and sinker!

His heart pounding wildly, he shook his head and tried to focus. *Come on, get a grip, Preston. It's only a girl.* But no matter how much he tried to convince himself, he couldn't take his eyes off her.

"Preston, what are they talking about in there?" Paige asked. "Preston?"

Snapping out of his girl-induced coma, he hadn't the slightest clue of what she'd just asked. "Uh, wha...what did you say?" he asked, trying to keep one eye on the girl and the other on his sister.

Annoyed, Paige stared narrowly at him. "Never mind—so, what are you looking at?" Shrugging, he turned his attention back to the lecture hall as she scowled and postured herself for a fight. "It's another girl, isn't it?"

Blindsided, his mouth fell open. "Hey, little girl, it's none of your business!" he said dismissively. "Anyway, I'm still trying to figure out what they're talking about."

"Uh-huh, sure—so why are you drooling all over yourself," she asked sharply, "huh?"

Determined to continue the battle as a matter of principle, Preston prepared to launch a counter attack, when a blinding flash went off from inside the auditorium. "What was that?" he yelled, putting his nose to the glass. "Mom, what happened?" Shaking her head, she glanced at him, stammering as she stood there.

Through the door, Preston gazed at the tall, sandy-haired instructor. Clad in a blood-red buckskin duster, he stood in the center of the room, pointing to the upper level seats. Launching a fiery red orb from his hand, he fired it at a boy in the back row. Swiftly, the kid sprang to his feet and threw his hands out in front of him as he tried to protect himself within a blanket of turquoise energy. Seconds later, the fireball hit the half-baked shield, knocking the flustered boy back into his seat.

Glued to the window, Preston and Paige followed the precept's every move as Natewick came up behind them. "Oh, where has the time gone? If we're to have any time to meet the chancellor, I'm afraid we'll have to bypass the playing fields."

Preston winced at the news, letting out a sigh as the rooftop bell rang. Immediately, a flood of students poured out from the classrooms, filling the hall with a sea of green uniforms. In the blink of an eye, thoughts of Pryttonn and playing fields flew from his mind as he searched for the girl. Bit by bit, the palms of his hands began to sweat and his heart raced, when suddenly, he saw her.

Ready to use every ounce of charm he could conjure up, Preston watched her every step as she approached him. Staring into her golden eyes, he tried to speak, but to his horror, the words came out in a stream of mindless babble. *No! What am I doing? This can't be happening!*

Gasping for air and sinking fast, he backed away, but instead, stumbled and fell to the floor. Mortified, he cracked open an eye, hoping the girl would be gone, but to his unending shame, he found her gazing curiously down at him.

"Preston? What are you doing on the floor?" his mom asked, stomping all over his moment of pure bliss. "Get up and stop clowning around, we've got to go."

Geez, it's bad enough that I look like a total idiot, but now my mom!

Getting to his feet, he flashed a smile at the dazzling girl. "Uh, I'm Preston, what's—"

"Preston, come on," his mom shouted. "Let's go—now!" Clinging to the smallest thread of hope, he shot a disapproving glance at her, but as he turned back toward the girl, she was gone.

On the way back to Manderlane Hall, Preston kicked himself every step of the way, as Paige and Natewick chattered back and forth. *At least I got to talk to her, sort of. But I don't even know her name,* he thought. *I guess I'll never know. Man, can things get any worse than this? Yeah, they probably can.*

"Mrs. Brandymire, ya'll be heading up to the fourth floor,"

Natewick instructed as she stepped into the elevator. "While ya're busy upstairs, I'll keep a close eye on Paige and Preston." As the doors slid open, she peeked out into the deserted lobby where the embers of a fire cracked and popped in an open hearth. Shadows danced across the engraved walls as she walked to the far side of the room and peered down a dim hallway.

Strange, this hall seems to go on forever. Making her way down the long corridor, she moved in and out of the soft light, then came to a dead end. "Where are the doors?" Puzzled, she shook her head and turned back. "Is there anything about this place that isn't strange?"

"Well, to be honest—no," a voice answered, "but on the other hand, there's never a dull moment around here either."

Startled, she spun around, only to find a man standing in front of a doorway. "What? Where in the world did you come from? There wasn't a—"

"A door?" he asked with a boyish grin. "Uh, it's nothing more than a security measure. After all, one can't likely get into a room that has no doors or windows, can they?"

Uneasily, she stared into his emerald eyes, and then at the crescent birthmark on his neck. *That mark – my kids have the same one.* Unnerved, a warm, prickly sensation washed over her as she followed him into his office.

"Welcome to Raydencrafft. I'm Mathias Manderlane, the conservatory's chancellor," he said, pulling a chair out for her, "and you must be Mrs. Brandymire—I've heard quite a lot about your children."

Quickly, her eyes darted around the room, coming to rest on a portrait that hung behind the chancellor's desk. *The statue in the library's garden – it's the same man.* Below the portrait, a warm fire burned in a stone fireplace. On the mantle, a long glass case held a dark green gun-metal staff. *A staff—a little medieval, isn't it? What is this place? And why do they want my kids?*

"As you know, the school year is already in full swing. So, the situation requires that I cut straight to the chase," he said seriously. "How soon can your children begin their studies here with us?"

"Excuse me?" she blurted out. Jumping up, she put a chair between them as a barrier. "Wait a minute—aren't we getting a little ahead of ourselves?"

He leaned forward in his chair and smiled. "I apologize for my bluntness," he said, running a fast hand through his auburn hair. "I realize you must have quite a few questions and some reservations too, that's understandable."

"Questions—reservations?" she exclaimed, shaking her head. "You're kidding, right?"

"Mrs. Brandymire, believe me, I want the same thing that you want for your children. They deserve an atmosphere where they're not treated as outcasts," he said emphatically. "Raydencrafft may not be an ordinary school by any stretch of the imagination, but here they'll have thousands of students, precepts and staff members around them that share similar gifts as they do. Now, regarding the subject of tuition—"

Okay, great, here it comes, she mused. *Money—money—money. Yeah, I knew this was too good to be true.*

"Head Counsel Beadle expressed your concerns over the financial aspects of enrolling your children here," he said, pulling a folder from his desk. "Frankly, I don't want the issue of money to deter us, so I've taken the liberty of having him speak to some of our wealthier alumni and patrons." As he thumbed through the folder, she bit her lip, trying to read the paperwork upside down. "In short, we've made arrangements for a sponsorship of sorts, wherein their tuition would be paid by a benefactor who wishes to remain anonymous. This, of course, includes room and board, plus all necessary supplies and materials for the duration of their time with us."

Almost in tears, she sat back down in her chair, and tried to grasp what she'd heard. "Uh, I'm not sure what to say—I'd like to talk to my husband first and give you our decision tomorrow," she said, trembling in her seat.

What's to discuss? Everything's been taken care of. And a secret benefactor? Who would have ever imagined it?

Chapter Seven

A Nightmarish Beginning

RUN! The frantic thought rang in Paige's mind. *RUN!* Through the high brush and down the rocky footpath, she ran as fast as she could, the rain pelting her from every direction. Above, the night sky raged, keeping pace with her every step. Terrified, she stopped and looked back. *Where is She? I can't see her!* CRACK! Hearing the sound, she bolted down the trail, cutting herself on the bushes along the way. As she reached a fork in the path, she stood there frozen in place. *I don't know which way to go – which way?*

Blood and tears streamed down her face as she tried desperately to think. *I can't breathe – it hurts so much.* SNAP! Forcing herself to choose, she cut through the overgrowth, then stopped and stared up the steep mountainside. *Is that somebody calling my name?* Veering off the trail, she hid in the bushes, straining her eyes to see. "Help me," she cried. "*She's* after me! Please!"

"Paige," a voice called out, "this way!"

Amid a relentless torrent, she fought her way up to the cliffs. "Where are you?" she screamed. "Say something!" All of a sudden, she stumbled and slid down the hill, grinding to a stop. Covered in mud, she struggled to her feet and ran up the rise as lightning lit the hillside. *There's someone up there!* "Wait, I'm down here!" Groping her way to the top, she dropped to her knees, sobbing. *I saw someone here. I know I didn't imagine it, I couldn't have.*

"Paige, up here," the voice bellowed out from somewhere up ahead, "there's a passageway, hurry!"

She looked out over the edge, then turned back towards the trail. *I don't know what to do, but I can't go back.* Reaching the opening, she peered inside, but could only see a short distance. "Why are you doing this? Who are you?"

"You know who I am," the voice echoed. "You've known all along."

Pulling her Laurelean Bloom from her pocket, she held the glowing stone in front of her. Step by step, she moved forward, keeping a constant watch behind her. Around her, a warm mist filled the air as it snaked its way through the endless maze. *I'm so tired. I can't do this anymore.*

Once again, the voice beckoned. "Paige—keep moving, it's not much farther."

"Not much farther?" she cried, forcing herself to go on. "Where am I going?" CRASH! SMASH! Spinning around, her eyes focused on the footpath. *It's impossible, how could She find me so fast?* In a panic, she scrambled up the tunnel, then slipped and hit the ground hard. *The stone—I dropped it! I can't see anything!* Fighting to her feet, she felt her way through the blackness, when out of the blue, a blast of cool air brushed past her. *It must be a way out, it's got to be!* Blindly, she moved in the direction of the gusting wind, probing her way along the walls. Reaching the top of a sharp incline, she stood there gazing out over an enormous canyon. *No! It's a dead end! What am I going to do?*

"The way is barred and time grows short—use the key you possess," the voice echoed, "only then will you find the answer. Remember, it lies hidden in the darkness—in the darkness."

"Wait! What key? I don't know what to do! Come back, don't leave me here!" Trembling, she fell to her knees as freezing rain poured in from the opening, stinging her skin like a thousand needle pricks. *I don't know what to do—I just wish I hadn't lost my bloom.* "All this happens," she whispered, "and all I can think of is a stupid rock."

Suddenly, the shrill sound of mad screeching bellowed from the passage as it lit up in indigo. Out of it came a rolling horror heading straight for her. With no time to react, it hit her head-on, hurling her over the edge of the cliff into the black abyss.

Plunging—spinning—falling down—down into a bottomless void, she desperately fought to free herself from the fiery web that ensnared her as the woman's scornful shrieks echoed from above. Rapidly, the cliff disappeared from view, and just as quick, the ground came rushing toward her.

With a blood-curdling scream, Paige shot up from her bed drenched in sweat, causing a three-way collision between her roommates as they jumped from their berths in a stupor. "Huh? What happened?" one of them asked. Another shrugged as Paige looked down at them from her upper bunk.

"Sorry, I must've had a nightmare," she said timidly.

Rolling their eyes, the three girls climbed back into bed as Paige rubbed her face and squinted at the clock. *Three in the morning! I can't go back to sleep again, what if I have another nightmare?* Gazing at the painted sky on the ceiling, she counted the stars one by one. *I can't believe we're here at Raydencrafft, it feels like a dream. But it can't be – I just woke up from one.* Laying her head back on her pillow, she pulled the blankets up around her and stared out the window. *I really miss Mom and Dad, it was hard to say goodbye to them.*

Actually, the only good thing she could say about their first day was that Natewick took the time to walk them to their quarters. Much to her relief, he even stayed to introduce them to their overseers. Overseers, he explained, were responsible for watching over certain areas of the conservatory. In this case, the sleeping chambers and lounges that they would call home for the next six months.

Late that afternoon, Thayne Wescombe, Preston's floor overseer, greeted them at the entrance of the boy's building. Tall and stocky like a linebacker, he had steel gray eyes that gave him a menacing appearance. As was the custom around school, he wore the traditional forest-green uniform. On his cuffs were the traditional gray-colored braids of his order, but a third silver braid ran between them. Platinum insignia fashioned to match the small marks on his neck, which resembled wisps of wind, adorned his jacket collar.

"Hello, Thayne. I hope ya don't mind, but I thought I'd come along to make sure these two got settled in," Natewick said cheerfully. "This is Preston Brandymire and his sister Paige."

"Hello there, it's good to meet you both," he said, shaking their hands. "Why don't we head inside and get Preston set up?" As they walked down the hallway, several boys jockeyed for position outside the first floor lounge, while others poked their heads out from their rooms. Much like a game of telephone, murmurs of crescents spread through the group as Preston wrinkled his nose at them and walked up the stairs.

"All right, keep it down," Thayne barked as they entered the rowdy second floor lounge. "These are your new classmates—Preston and Paige Brandymire." Again, the boys chattered among themselves, but quickly, he cut them short. "Guys, be nice—stop horsing around."

Timidly, Paige peeked out from behind Preston as the boys primped and preened themselves, shoving one another in a vain attempt to gain her attention. Shaking his head, Preston smirked at her. "Can you believe this? What a bunch of clowns. I'd never do that, uh-uh," he muttered as her eyes widened in disbelief.

Pulling three boys from the group, Thayne whispered to them, and then they each grinned as if they'd won a prize. "Okay, Preston, you're in chamber 2-27. These guys are your roommates." Pointing to the tallest of the three, he cracked a smile. "That's Aaron Clement, our resident Pryttonn expert. And at thirteen, that's quite a feat."

"Hey Preston," Aaron said, pulling his cap down over his wavy brown hair. "Don't listen to him. He always piles it on way too thick."

"Yeah—yeah—yeah, whatever," Thayne countered as he put his hands on the shoulders of a short, squatty, strawberry-haired kid. "Uh, this troublemaker's Jim Richardson. You'd better watch out for him, because he's every precept's worst nightmare, day or night."

Jim scowled at him, then shined a mouthful of braces at Preston as Thayne waved over the last boy. "Now, on to this big guy—meet Wil Buller," he said as Wil gave Preston a giant-sized grin, "the genuine apple of Precept Dryden's eye."

"Hey, that's not funny," Wil said, brushing his straight blond hair from his face. "I'm not the apple of anything."

With a crooked smile, Preston chuckled as Natewick tapped him on the shoulder. "Preston, now that ya're settled in and all, this might be an opportune time for me and Paige to slip away," the little man said as Paige did her best to hide her anxiety.

"Ummm, Mr. Wescombe? Since it's our first day, can I walk my sister over to her building?" Preston asked, glancing at his roommates and then Paige. "I'll be right back, I swear."

"Sure, no problem, we'll go over the house rules when you get back—see you in a few."

Heaving a sigh of relief, Paige followed Natewick and Preston through the ever watchful horde of boys, exhaling when they finally reached the exit. "I'm sorry, Preston, I guess I'm still a little nervous."

"Come on, there's nothing to be sorry about. Besides, I'm nervous too. I promise we'll see each other at breakfast tomorrow, okay?" At the girl's quarters, they made their way up to the third floor, and stopped by the lounge. Peering inside, Preston frowned. "Man, it's as quiet as a tomb in here—boring." Down at the end of the hall, a few girls ran for cover while a small group hung out near the library. Playfully, he winked at them, chuckling as they scattered like field mice. "Uh, I guess I better go. Mr. Beadle, thanks for staying—and Paige, relax, I'll see you in the morning."

Looking as if she might toss up her dinner, she waved at him. "Goodnight—remember, you promised."

"Don't worry, I won't forget," he said as he bolted down the stairs.

"Allrighty, let's meet your overseer," Natewick said as they stopped by the door marked *Mesheleine Temberly, O.B.S., GIRL'S OVERSEER.* Knocking softly, they waited for a few seconds, then out came a pretty girl in her late-teens. Towering over them, she had fiery amber eyes and an olive complexion which probably made her stand out everywhere she went.

"Oh, Head Counsel Beadle, I must have gotten my wires crossed, I thought you'd be here a little later."

"Well, yes—this little lassie arrived early," he said, patting Paige on the shoulder. "Ummm, missy, this is Mesheleine."

"Hi, it's nice to meet you," Paige said, gazing at the gleaming sun-shaped insignia on her jacket, "I'm Paige."

"Hey there, you can call me Meshel for short," she said, waving them in. Straightening up, she draped her jacket over the back of a chair as Paige sat down across from her.

"Missy, I think I'll leave ya two to talk," Natewick said. "Meshel, it's a pleasure as always. Remember, this little lassie's a special one, so ya take real good care of her." She gave him a quick nod, and with a wink, he slipped out the door.

"So, I'm sure you'll want to meet your roommates," Meshel said, pulling out a floor-plan. "Hmmm, let's see…ummm, 3-17. Yeah, I think you'll fit in nicely there."

Oh my gosh, what if I don't fit in? Paige fretted. *What if they don't like me?*

"Okay, let's go meet the girls," Meshel said as she stepped into the hallway, "I know they'll flip when they see you." Near the end of the hall, she stopped at their bedchamber, knocking as Paige shuffled nervously in one spot. As they walked inside, a girl smiled at them from one of the lower bunks as the two other girls turned their attention away from the computer.

"Girls, meet Paige Brandymire, your new roommate," she said, gesturing at the chubby, nerdy looking girl lying on the bed. "Paige, that's Terrin Matthews, this floor's math wiz. But stay out of her way if she has a book in her hand, she's an accident waiting to happen in the body of a ten year old."

"Hi Paige," Terrin said, swiping her stringy, dirty-blonde hair from her face, "and by the way, she's exaggerating."

"Yeah, right, if you say so," Meshel said, patting the head of a black-haired beanpole of a kid. "*This* is Aubree Stemson, Precept Grievley's pet project."

Avoiding the girl's violet glare, Meshel explained that Aubree was the precept's *go-to girl* whenever he couldn't get an answer from the dull-witted students he pointed to. This knack of answering any question thrown her way came to be affectionately known around school as *'the Aubree effect.'* Despite the legions of humiliated students the eleven year old left in her wake, Aubree hadn't a clue as to why she had trouble making friends.

"Relax, Aubree, I'm just pulling your chain," Meshel said as Aubree stared awkwardly at Paige, then gave her a brace filled grin. Chuckling, Meshel nudged the girl next to her. "All right, last but not least, this is Elise, my kid sister *and* our tomboy. When it comes to sports, she can beat the pants off of any boy."

"Meshel's right, I've seen it," Aubree said, jabbing Elise in the side. "She's a great batter too. You'll see when the Pryttonn tryouts come around."

"Aubree, I'm not even close to being that good," Elise said, pulling her long golden-brown hair back into a ponytail. "Anyway, it's nice meeting you Paige."

Paige gazed around the room as Meshel poked her head out into the hall, then turned to look at her sister. "Elise, try to help Paige out as much as you can, explain the rules and such, okay? Well, I have to do my rounds now. Remember, lights out at nine-thirty."

As she left, they eyeballed each other until Terrin broke the ice by way of a verbal wrecking ball. "So Paige, you're a crescent, huh?" she asked bluntly as the other girl's mouths fell open. "Funny, I could have sworn the chancellor was the only crescent here. Aubree, aren't they supposed to be rare?"

Wincing, Aubree sputtered as Paige and Elise stared uneasily at Terrin, who in turn continued her rather unsubtle idea of small talk. "So, what can you do," she asked with curiosity, "huh?"

What can I do? Paige thought as she frowned at the nerdy girl. *She makes it sound as if I can flip things on like a light switch.*

Elise glared at Terrin and cut her off at the pass. "I really don't think Paige wants to talk about this right now, she's probably tired, right?"

"Oh, shoot, I'm sorry," Terrin said as she did an about face. "I should have kept my big mouth shut."

With a smile, Paige patted her on the shoulder. "Don't worry about it," she said tactfully. "Besides, you should ask someone else, because I'm totally clueless about this stuff."

"Clueless?" Aubree blurted out. "I'd give my pest of a little brother away to be a crescent. I mean, being a green leaf is nice, but to be *that* special—I'd hand him over in a second."

Paige wrinkled her nose in mild annoyance. "Special? Well, it's brought me and my brother nothing but grief," she said flatly. "So, I'll take ordinary any day."

"Wait a minute, you mean, there are *two* of you?" Aubree asked, gawking at her. "I don't believe it, what are the chances?"

"Chances? What are you talking about?" Paige asked, shaking her head. "Anyway, you'll get to meet Preston tomorrow at breakfast—but I still don't see what the big deal is."

As if lightning had struck her, Elise gazed wide-eyed at Paige. "Wait, what did you say your brother's name was? Did you say—Preston?"

"Uh-huh, why?" Paige asked, raising a brow at her.

"Oh, no reason, I just thought I'd heard that name before," she said coyly. "It must have been on TV or something."

Shrugging her shoulders, Paige glanced at the sleeping berths. "So, I guess that one's mine," she said, pointing to the neatly made top bunk. "Which set of drawers do I get?"

"These," Terrin said, tapping them. "Hey, I'm still hungry. Anyone want to get a snack?"

Paige grabbed a bowl full of grapes and a bottle of water, then followed them to the lounge and sat down near the fire. Across the room, three other girls sat glued to the TV, hanging on every word that came from it.

"Ummm, Paige, so how old is your brother?" Elise asked.

Breaking away from the TV trio, Paige looked at her with growing curiosity. "He just turned thirteen," she said, popping a grape into her mouth, "but he tries to act a lot older than he really is."

"So, what does he do for fun?" she asked. "You know, like hobbies and stuff."

Paige's eyes narrowed. "I don't know, he's got baseball on the brain—and video games, too. Uh, why are you so interested in him?"

Lightheartedly, Elise giggled as she changed the subject. "Oh, it's almost nine-thirty," she said, getting up from the couch. "We'd better go."

Finishing the last of her grapes, Paige downed her water and waited as Aubree and Terrin gathered their things. Glancing at the wall clock, she stared curiously at the girls watching TV. "Aubree, those girls—why aren't they leaving? Won't they get in trouble?"

"Oh, yeah, they will. Randi and her princess posse always try to push their luck with Meshel," Aubree said flatly. "Because they're shooting stars, she thinks they can get away with it, being telepathic and all, but they never do. They usually get house detention and wind up cleaning the whole lounge after class. It's dumb if you ask me."

On the way back to their chamber, Paige mulled over what Aubree had said, when Elise snuck up behind her. "Paige?" she asked softly. "Does he have a girlfriend?"

Nearly tripping over herself, Paige spun around. "Who…what?" she whispered. "You mean Preston? I don't know." Elise moaned as she threw her a pitiful look. "Okay—okay, I'm pretty sure he doesn't have one." *Preston – it figures.*

As the nine-thirty chimes sounded, they hurried inside, got ready for bed, then climbed into their berths. Quietly, Paige pulled the covers up over her, and drifted off to sleep, unaware of the nightmare to come.

I can't get back to sleep, Paige thought. *I swear I'm going to be the class zombie tomorrow, I just know it. Everyone's going to think I'm a total delinquent.* Rubbing her eyes, she sighed as she gazed out the window at the full moon. *How can I sleep if I keep thinking about that horrible dream? Which way is barred? And what key? I don't get it at all.* Desperately, she struggled to stay awake, but finally fell asleep, this time in a peaceful slumber.

Chapter Eight

The Girl With the Golden Eyes

Tick-tock—tick-tock—BRR_RING! Like a hammer striking a steel drum, the alarm rattled through Paige's brain. Blurry-eyed and semi-comatose, she launched from her bed, and tried to focus on Aubree, but could only see a fuzzy blob.

"Crud, you look horrible," Aubree said, sandwiching her face in her hands. "What time did you get to sleep?"

Keeping one eye shut and squinting out the other, Paige watched as the blob slowly turned into a fuzzy version of Aubree. "Uh, about four-thirty, I think," she said, sliding down from her berth, "but it's still kind of foggy."

Terrin stared wide-eyed at Paige, then smirked at Aubree and Elise. "Boy, I don't know, we might have to drag her to class. By the way, what was your nightmare about anyway?"

After running through a bunch of jumbled answers in her head, Paige spilled out the one that made the most sense. Halfway through her story, Aubree brought things to a sudden halt. "Hey, where'd those come from?" On the desk sat a set of books, a class schedule and a note, all tied together with an emerald green satin ribbon.

"Paige, it's a hand written message from the chancellor, for you," Terrin said excitedly as Aubree and Elise squeezed in for a closer look. Untying the bow, Paige picked up the note, and read it out loud.

Dear Paige:

I wanted to drop you a note to say how pleased I am that you're here at the conservatory. I look forward to meeting you and your brother after you've both had a chance to settle in. It's my sincere wish that you will find your time here most fulfilling.

These books are for the current trimester. I hope they'll be to your liking. I have taken the liberty of including a couple of my own personal volumes that I think you'll enjoy.
My best,

Mathias Manderlane

Chancellor Mathias Manderlane
P.S.: Don't fear your dreams or the darkness, many answers can be found there.

Stopping short of the postscript, Paige eyes darted around the room. *Dreams? Darkness? But how could he know? Oh, now that's just plain creepy.*

"You're so lucky," Aubree griped. "I don't think any of us have ever gotten a letter from him."

Paige stared at the note as Elise and Terrin checked out her class schedule. "Hey, you're in my second period class," Terrin said gleefully, "and we've all got Esoteric-Studies #3 for fourth period."

Feeling less like a zombie and more like someone who'd been hit by lightning, Paige stood there in a daze as the girls continued to chatter. "Oh, it's almost seven," Elise said. "Finish getting dressed, we've got to go."

On the way to the dining hall, Terrin and Aubree sparred over what to eat while Elise appeared to have something completely different on her mind. "Paige, are you sure your brother's meeting us this morning, he said he would, didn't he?"

"Yes, he did," Paige said grudgingly. "I promise, you'll get to meet him soon, okay?" Inside, she searched the packed tables for Preston, but couldn't pick him out of the crowd. "I forgot how big this place was. Let's get our food first, and maybe we'll see him in line."

"Paige!" Preston shouted from the middle of the crowd. "Paige—over here!" Craning her neck, she followed his voice until she found him. In chorus, the girls grabbed their trays and weaved through the feeding frenzy, reaching his table with one final push.

"Sis, you remember these guys, don't you?" he asked, gesturing to his roommates. "Hey guys, let's make some space." Smirking, he swung his legs over the bench and jumped up, only to find himself standing nose to nose with Elise.

Silent and numb, he stared at her, then sputtered as Wil elbowed him and made a face. "Uh, Preston, I think the word you're trying to find is *hello.*"

Terrin and Aubree glanced at Paige as she threw a puzzled look at Elise, who seemed to be in a world of her own. *Oh, how pathetic can they get,* Paige thought as she shook her head. "Aren't you guys going to say anything? This is getting really boring."

Flipping her hair around, Elise brought Preston back to reality and gazed into his eyes. "Ummm, the last time I saw you, weren't you on the floor?" she asked. "I hope you didn't hurt yourself."

Preston squirmed as he cleared his throat. "Oh...uh, that day was sort of a blur."

"Well, I'm sorry I couldn't stay," she said, biting her lip. "I really wanted to, but things didn't—well, you know."

Rubbing his face, he gave her a wily grin. "Hey, it's okay, but I've got to ask you something. What's your name?"

"Oops—sorry, I'm Elise," she said with a nervous giggle. Blushing, she pointed toward her roommates. "And these are my friends, Aubree and Terrin." Quickly, the two girls waved and turned back to their meals, and then everyone began to chat back and forth as they all finished breakfast.

BRR_RING! As everybody grabbed their things, Preston smiled at Paige. "So you have English next, right? Talk about a snorefest," he said as she let out a big yawn. "Whoa, what did you guys do, stay up all night?"

"No," she said, slipping her backpack on. "I just couldn't sleep."

Glumly, Preston stared at her. "Uh, don't feel bad, I had a rotten night too. I woke up at three after a whopper of a nightmare."

"Three o'clock?" Paige asked, her eyes growing as wide as saucers. "Are you sure it was three?"

"Yeah—why?" he asked, dividing his attention between her

and Elise.

"Uh, no reason—so, what was your dream about?"

"I don't know, it's kinda fuzzy in parts," he said, trying to recall the details. "You were in it, and so was that nutty glob-of-goo."

Shocked, Paige sputtered as her mouth fell open. "What? What else do you remember?"

"Uh, it was raining in the hills…no…the mountains," he said, running his hands through his hair. "I ran into this really dark tunnel. I could hear you, but when I tried to find you, I couldn't. Then I heard another voice. It said something about a key, and that I had to find something else, you know, blah-blah-whatever."

"That's it?" she said flabbergasted. "Blah-blah-whatever?"

Frowning, he wrinkled his nose at her. "Okay…okay, everything kinda lit up around me, and then I saw a whole bunch of tunnels and a big pit in the center of a weird temple or something. Oh, and remember that light? Well, that glowing-blob-of-whatever-*She*-is threw a big blue ball of flame at me," he said, slamming his fist into his other hand. "And just like that—BAM! I got knocked straight into that pit and woke up."

Giving Paige a sheepish grin, he hopped up the steps of the instructional hall as Elise and the others walked inside. "We'd better hurry," he said, peering through the doors. "Wait a minute, why are you so interested in my dream, anyway?"

Paige smiled coyly at him and shook her head. "Uh, I'm not—well, I'll see you after school."

Working her way upstairs, she stopped near her classroom. *This can't be a coincidence. But, we couldn't have been in the same dream, could we? Maybe it's some sort of a weird riddle—that must be what it is.*

"Nobody's going to believe this, not even Preston," she said under her breath. "Think, Paige, think. I've got to figure this out before something worse happens."

Chapter Nine

The Detention King

"So, you still too chicken to ask Elise to a movie?" Jim whispered in Preston's ear. "Oh, don't tell me, you hope she'll ask you first so you don't have to, I'm right, aren't I?"

Wanting to fire back, Preston glanced at the instructor and choked back the urge. *If I open my mouth in the middle of class again, it'll be suicide.* In the short time Preston had known him; Jim had managed to earn five detentions, which had to be a school record for sure. And, if you happened to be near him at ground zero, he'd take you down with him.

Just last week, Jim had hatched a scheme to pull off what he called a *mind* game, which used a shooting star ability he claimed would be fool-proof. The plan was simple—*persuade* Precept Grievley to trash the pop quiz he intended to give. "Hey, it'll be a snap. Besides, I'll be performing a public service," he said. In truth, it might have worked, if not for Aubree, who'd pointed a finger at Jim after she'd fished the quiz out of the trash.

The next day, Jim got slapped with a two hour detention, and then for good measure, Preston got the same for talking to him during class. Although earning detention was hardly new to Preston, serving one along side Jim had proved to be a special treat. For he was the only kid Preston had ever seen get detention while in detention.

"Okay, I guess you don't want to talk about Elise," Jim muttered. "So what else can we talk about?"

Rolling his eyes, Preston stared straight ahead, finally caving in under the barrage of endless babble. "Jim, I don't want to get in trouble again," he said quietly. "So shut your trap."

"Well, sure...fine, but I want to hear the *magic* word," Jim grumbled, "and that's *please.* So, what's it gonna be? Either you say it or I keep talking."

"All right—*please.* There, I said it, now shut up."

Crossing his arms, Jim brooded as Preston turned his attention back to the lecture. Only it was a bit too late. "Mr. Brandymire, is there something you wish to share with the rest of us?" Vice-Precept Lumenayre asked dryly as the entire class focused on him. "I'm sure your classmates wouldn't want to be left out, now would they?" As she gazed at him, he fidgeted in the hot seat, the color draining from his face. "It must have been important enough for you to interrupt my lecture—so, by all means, let's hear it."

Oh, crud. What am I going to say? She'll see right through me. "Uh, I...ummm," he said, sputtering as Jim tried to act like he'd had nothing to do with it at all. Taking a deep breath, Preston sank down into his seat and gripped the hand rests, when all of a sudden, the fire alarm sounded. Instantly, the building emptied as students funneled down the stairs. Outside, Preston glared at Jim. "You know, I could have used some help in there, I was sinking fast."

"Hey, I kinda thought I did pretty good, considering what I had to work with," Jim said proudly as he pointed a finger at Preston. "Face it—you just don't get the *finer side* of being a shooting star."

"Finer side? Now I've heard everything," Preston said heatedly. "I've seen your finer side plenty of times—it's about as subtle as a nuclear bomb."

Wincing at the comment, Jim scowled. "Fine, be ungrateful. Do whatever you want—it's no skin off my back."

"Ungrateful?" Preston asked in amazement. "What are you talking about?"

Jim gave him a sly look. "The alarm—I set it off. I caught some little sixth grader heading to the bathroom, so I *told* her to pull the alarm."

"What? Are you nuts?" Preston whispered. "You can't do that—if you get caught, we'll both get in trouble."

Staring uneasily at him, Jim drummed a finger against his forehead. "Okay, maybe I didn't think it all the way through, but there wasn't a lot of time to come up with something," he explained. "Besides, things weren't looking so good for you in there. Man, I thought you'd understand."

Preston grabbed a handful of hair and forced out an uneasy smile. "Jim, I know you meant well, but you've got to stop doing this. I can't afford to get expelled again."

"Again? Whoa! You never mentioned that before," he said, starting to laugh. "What did you do? Forget your lunch or something?"

"Uh, it's a long story," Preston said, tapping the crescent on his neck, "but this was the main reason."

Getting the picture, Jim frowned. "Yeah—in elementary school, I used to ace every test I took. I got away with it for awhile, but then I got accused of cheating, and well, I was—sort of, if you know what I mean. So when middle school came around, I wound up here."

Preston sighed as he glanced at the entrance where a group of precepts gathered. "I think they've figured out it was a false alarm. If they start a search-and-destroy mission to find out who did it, we're sunk."

Smirking, Jim shook his head. "Hey, I wouldn't worry about it—you're too much of a do-gooder to get expelled. Besides, if I haven't gotten kicked out of school yet, why should you?"

In a really strange way, what Jim said made sense, but as they walked back into the lecture hall, reality came crashing down on them. Standing there in her burnt-orange overdress, Vice-Precept Lumenayre followed their every move, staring them down as they slid into their seats.

"Mr. Brandymire and Mr. Richardson, I'd like to speak with you before you leave," she said coldly as the bell rang, "the rest of the class is dismissed." At a snail's pace, Preston and Jim weaved through a grim procession of classmates, each gazing at them as if they were the guests of honor at a funeral.

"Gentlemen, I know you were talking during my lecture, am I correct?" Cringing, they both nodded in tandem. "Good—no lies thus far. I do enjoy a refreshing bit of honesty, don't you?" she asked, shifting her fiery amber glare to Jim. "But somehow, I'm quite certain that *you* had more to do with it than Mr. Brandymire." Looking absolutely numb, Jim wilted. "Oh, and wait, I almost forgot to mention the fire alarm—*that* was very clever. Well, the next time you decide to use your misspent abilities to manipulate a fellow classmate into breaking the rules, you'll wish you hadn't, I guarantee it."

Studying their expressions, she paced the room, then stopped and ran a hand along her ebony neck. "Now, I wouldn't want you to think that I'm not serious," she said sternly. "So, two hours detention for Mr. Brandymire and *three* hours for you, Mr. Richardson—report to Miss Picklesimer at seven o'clock tonight in the main library. You'll be cleaning the basements, is that clear?"

Stunned, their mouths dropped open as Jim began to sputter. "But...it's lights out at nine-thirty—I won't get finished until ten."

Raising a brow, she shook her head. "That's regrettable, but these rules are in place for a reason. If you break them, someone could get hurt," she said emphatically. "Consider yourself fortunate that this wasn't the case today. You may not be so lucky in the future." Leading the boys toward the exit, she stopped at the door and threw them a cold smile. "I'll have your overseer escort you back to your chamber at the end of each of your detention periods," she said, pushing them out into the hall. "Oh, and I hope you both have a *pleasant* day."

Chapter Ten

The Charming Miss Picklesimer

With his bag overburdened by a mind-boggling load of homework, Preston halfheartedly made his way back to his quarters. The rest of the day had gone okay, but the way he and Jim had left things bothered him. *I shouldn't have ragged on him the way I did, but now I've got bigger problems. How can I finish all this homework and serve a detention in the same night? It's impossible.*

Running up the stairs and into the study hall, Preston stared keenly at the wall clock. *Four-thirty? There isn't enough time.* Reluctantly, he dumped out the contents of his bag, and winced at the pile. *Candy wrappers and leftover jerky sticks, what a mess.* Tossing them in the trash, he frowned as he pulled a wad of gum off one of his assignments. "Great—gum and homework, I've really got to stop doing this."

Plowing through one assignment after another, Preston crammed what he'd finished into his binder when Aaron poked his head in. "So, this is where you've been hiding out," he said, gawking at the jumbled stack of paper. "Crud, how much homework do you have? This all can't be from today, can it?"

Preston sighed, but kept writing. "Yeah, it makes me want to gag," he moaned. "I swear Precept Grievley's got it out for me. *Four* pages on indigenous trees, can you believe it? I've got to write out a description on each one, and if that's not enough, I have to draw their leaf patterns, too. I'd pass out from the boredom if I wasn't so afraid of failing."

Aaron sifted through the unfinished pages and made a face. "Uh, I probably shouldn't bring this up, but I think the whole school heard about the fire alarm today," he said tactfully, "and from the way Jim's acting, it sure looks like he had something to do with it."

"Something to do with it? He had everything to do with it," Preston said, slamming his pencil against the table. "And then I got in trouble for trying to make him shut his trap—so now we both have detention."

Backing off the subject, Aaron elbowed Preston, and gave him a good-natured grin. "Well, you're still going to eat, right? It's nearly five-thirty."

"Yeah, maybe I will," he said, shoveling the remaining homework into his bag. "I guess I'll finish the rest when I get back."

"Wil and Jim went to the dining hall already," Aaron said as they headed out the door, "but I've gotta warn you, Jim's not much for company."

A cloud of gloom hung over the table as Preston and Jim

picked at their dinner. Finally, Preston dropped his fork on his plate. "I just can't wait. Two hours with Miss Picklesimer, it's the perfect detention. Not only do we have to work, but she'll be nagging us while we're doing it."

Aggravated, Jim pushed his plate aside. "At least you only have two hours, I've got three," he griped, "and that basement, talk about a creepfest. Imagine it—cobwebs, rats, and a bunch of other things I don't even want to think about—that's what we're getting tonight."

Paige and Elise fidgeted as Aubree threw Jim a dismissive glance. "I think you're exaggerating," she said in an uppity voice that she'd all but mastered. "Miss Picklesimer isn't messy, and she's not a nag."

Jim and Preston rolled their eyes in unison. They both knew Aubree's opinion was that of the minority at school—a minority of one. Almost every kid knew that Miss Picklesimer was an absolute pain, no doubt about it. For more years than anyone cared to admit, she'd been the head librarian, an exceptional one by her own account. Never too bashful to tout her virtues, she enjoyed blowing her horn at every student that crossed her path, each and every time.

"Listen, you little snitch," Jim said, thumbing his nose at Aubree. "I don't remember asking for your opinion. Besides, what makes you think we even care about what you think of Miss Pickle-*slimer.*"

"You know, that's just plain mean," Aubree said, clinching her fists. "I didn't put that quiz in the trash, you did! Now I'm glad you got in trouble."

Preston stuck his fingers in his ears and glared at them. "Oh, come on, what difference does it make? She's right and you're right, okay? Geez, all I want is to get this night over with."

Staring defiantly at Jim, Aubree stewed as she sat there with her arms crossed, but at least the cease fire seemed to be holding. Well, maybe not. "And it's Pickle-*simer,* not Pickle-*slimer!"* she shouted. "You're such a jerk!"

Bewildered, Preston slapped his forehead, then turned to Jim and shrugged. "Uh, we'd better go," he said, flashing an uneasy grin. "If you guys don't hear from us by morning, send in a search party."

In silence, Jim and Preston walked slowly along the river, watching the moon inch its way above the horizon as twilight turned to night. Tiny swirls of milky light danced on the water as they approached the library and their impending plunge into utter boredom.

"Preston! Wait!" Paige yelled as she and Elise ran up behind them. Out of breath, she hunched over, putting her hands on her knees as Elise gazed coyly at Preston. "We weren't sure if we could catch up to you in time."

"Okay, but what are you guys doing out here?" Preston asked as Jim paced behind him. "Isn't it a little late for a field trip?"

"No, it's not even seven yet," Paige said as she looked up at the moon. "Anyway, Elise's sister said we could help you."

Preston smirked as he ran his hands through his hair. "Thanks for offering, but why should you have to work because of what we did?"

Instantly, Jim's mouth dropped open. "Hey, hold on a minute, if they're dumb enough to want to help, I'm not gonna stop them."

"Dumb? Uh, we're not here to help *you,"* Elise said doggedly. "Besides, it's our choice—all we need is Miss Picklesimer's permission."

Bewildered, Preston gave in and walked up to the entrance.

"All you need is her permission?" he asked in disbelief. "Sure...okay, good luck with that." Pressing the button on the library's brass intercom, he shuffled his feet while the others hid behind him.

All of a sudden, the head librarian's shrill voice blasted from the speaker. "Yes, who's there?" she asked, then answered herself. "Oh, yes, the vice-precept's problem students, I'll be right down."

Preston stared uneasily at the girls as Jim peered inside. "Ummm, you still have time to run before she gets here," Preston offered, "I wouldn't blame you if you did." Undaunted, they both shook their heads as he rolled his eyes at them. "You're nuts, you know that. Fine, if that's what you want, I can't stop you, but don't say I didn't warn you."

At last, the point of no return had come as Miss Picklesimer appeared at the door with her assistant. *Oh, great, it's Santa's demented wife and her twisted little Christmas elf,* Preston thought. *Uh, I really didn't need to see this.*

As the door opened, Elise made the first move. "Ummm, Miss Picklesimer?" she asked cautiously. "Can we help them clean up? My sister said it would be okay as long as we asked you."

The head librarian tapped her lips with her index finger. "Young lady, these boys are serving detention. This isn't a party—you do realize that, don't you?" Elise flashed Paige a look of worry, and then they both nodded. "Fine, you two can help," she said curtly, pointing at the boys, "but if I catch either of you shirking, they will receive double their current detention. That means no playing around—period. Do I make myself clear?" Sheepishly, the girls mumbled a quick yes. "Good—and that goes triple for you, Mr. Richardson." Jim shriveled up as she poked him in the shoulder. "I'd better not see any of your usual antics, understood?"

"Yes, Ma'am," Jim said feebly, dropping his head.

"Very well, then let's get started," she said, walking toward the stairs. "Follow me." Humming an odd tune, she guided them down into the depths of the library, finally stopping at the third level basement. Smugly, she smirked as Preston stared at the biggest pile of junk he'd ever seen. Rising up to the ceiling, a dank and dusty heap of old books and scrolls filled a large section of the basement. Piles of rusty armor and stacks of old paintings littered the narrow walkways, while scores of broken statues blocked others.

Great, I guess Mrs. Claus doesn't do housework, Preston thought. *She just has her elves sweep it down the stairs until it winds up down here.*

"I had hoped to get around to cleaning this up," the head librarian said as she cracked an evil grin, "but, my assistants and I have been far too busy. So, I find it fortunate that you have gotten in this much trouble."

Jim's eyes widened. "Can you believe this?" he whispered to Preston. "Vice-Precept Lumenayre really meant business, didn't she?"

"Yeah, she did," he said, scowling at him. "It's her rotten idea of fun—with an extra helping just for us."

SLAP! Clapping her hands together, Miss Picklesimer pointed a plump finger at the boys. "Pay attention! I don't wish to repeat myself," she screeched as Jim and Preston froze. "Now, as you can see, there's much to do down here. These walkways must be cleared and any loose items shelved." She walked back to the stairway and paused next to her assistant. "It's now seven-fifteen, my assistant will check on you from time to time. Remember, no playing around."

Jim grumbled and tossed his jacket on the floor as she disappeared up the stairs. "Man, I'd like to get my hands on Aubree's little pencil neck right now," he said, mimicking Aubree as he continued to rant. "Miss Picklesimer isn't a nag—blah-blah-blah. What a twerp! I should *make* her come down here and clean up this mess while I sit back and watch."

Unnerved, Preston glared at him. "Don't even think about it! Dark, dingy dungeons may be your thing, but they're not mine."

"Okay, fine," Jim snapped as he walked away. With a smirk, he scooped up a pile of armor, whistling as he carried it to the back of the room.

Shrugging at him, Preston looked at the girls. "Ummm, since he's doing the armor, I'll work on the paintings," he said, lifting a stack. "You guys can put the small stuff on those shelves or maybe sweep, whichever sounds better."

Nearly an hour had passed before Miss Picklesimer's assistant came scurrying down the stairs. Peering down the aisles, his eyes darted across the shelving, and stopped at Preston. "You and your friends need to work harder—you're falling behind," the little man barked. "This just won't do, the head librarian won't be pleased if this continues."

In a huff, he scuttled up the stairs as Preston dropped his stack of paintings and threw up his hands. "I don't believe this, we've been working for a solid hour and that's all the little gargoyle's got to say! Why doesn't he go back to the North Pole where he belongs? Not that they'd want him."

"Preston, it's all right, we'll get as much done as we can," Elise said softly, "I really don't mind."

Scooping up the paintings, Preston frowned. "Thanks, I guess I'm letting all this get to me," he said, staring awkwardly at her. "Elise, there's something I...uh, want to tell you, but I'm not sure what you'll think."

"What?" she asked as her face lit up. "Preston, tell me, I really want to know."

Oh, why did I have to open my big mouth? I can't do this. What if she thinks I'm a dork?

Struggling to find the right words, Preston choked back the nervous feeling in his stomach as Jim stepped between them. "Hey, I hate to interrupt your lovey-dovey gushfest," he said in jest, "but—OWWW!"

Preston kicked Jim in the shin, cutting him off before he could finish. "I'm sorry, but I can't stand it anymore," he blurted out. "Elise, I really like you—a lot. There—now you know."

Instantly, an awkward silence fell as Preston's heart sank. In that split second, he knew he'd crammed his entire foot into his mouth. Flustered, Elise glanced at Jim and Paige, and then around the basement as if she was trying to find a place to hide. "Well…uh…I like you too," she said uneasily. "I…ummm…uh—"

Preston's mind spun as he stepped back to regroup. "No, that's not what I meant—I mean I *really* like you, I have ever since I first saw you."

Elise picked up a painting and started to walk it to the back. Stopping, she turned in their direction. "Ummm, we'd better get back to work," she said, avoiding the stunned look on Preston's face, "there's more armor over here."

Weaving through the social wreckage that surrounded Preston, Jim and Paige hurried back to their work, leaving him standing there in misery. *I've gotta face it, I'm a complete moron,* Preston thought. *I don't have a clue of what I'm doing.* Moping his way to the back of the room, he dropped his armful of artwork and stared at Elise. *Great, she won't even look at me.*

He groaned, then walked towards the deepest section of the basement, trying to shake off the gloom hanging over him. *Boy, it's as cold as a meat locker back here, and it smells just as bad. Woof!* In the dim light, he gawked at the stacks of wooden crates that filled the walkways. "All right, I guess this is a good place to start."

Slowly, he lifted one box after another, working his way to the back wall where his lamp sat on a stack of boxes. Leaning against them, he wiped the sweat from his face, when, suddenly, the pile toppled over. SMASH! BANG! THUD! Preston hit the floor as the lantern shattered next to him. Tiny beams of light shot from the lamp as the glowflies scattered.

RUMBLE! WOOSH! With a gust of stale air, a portion of the wall rose into the ceiling, revealing a doorway. *A hidden passage? Oh, crud, I can barely see – those bugs are in too much of a hurry to get out of here.* Groping through the darkness, he inched his way to the nearest glowing lamp, pausing to look for the others. "Hey guys! You've got to see this," he shouted. "I found a creepy tunnel back here."

Rushing down one of the aisles, they ran up to Preston. "A tunnel?" Paige asked. "Where?"

Anxiously, Preston pointed behind him. "Back that way," he said, grabbing the nearby lantern. "But I've got to warn you, it smells really bad in there."

Reaching the opening, they all peeked in through the veil of cobwebs. "What do you think it's for?" Elise asked.

Preston shrugged as he scratched the side of his head, then set the lamp down. "You got me, but it seems like it hasn't been used for a long time," he said, stepping inside. "Whoa! It's way colder in here and it smells even worse."

Putting a hand to her nose, Paige watched him walk farther down the path. "Preston, you shouldn't be in there, I don't think it's a good idea. I mean, if it opened by itself, couldn't it close too?" she asked fretfully. "Uh, maybe we should tell Miss Picklesimer about it first."

"Tell Miss Picklesimer? No way," Jim said as he took a few

steps past Preston. "This is the best thing that's happened to us all night." Spewing out a string of eerie sounds, he smirked at the girls. "Come on, there's nothing scary in here. What are you guys—*chickens?"*

Paige's face turned beet red as she peered into the passage. "You know, I think Aubree's right, you are a complete jerk!"

"Oh, please, don't bring your little weasel of a friend into this," he said mockingly. "I don't waste my time on weasels, but for big chickens, I'll make an exception. So how's this? Buk-buk-BUK!"

Gritting her teeth, Paige glanced uneasily at Elise. "It can't be all that bad, can it?" she asked as Jim continued to egg them on.

"Jim, stop picking on them," Preston said as he jabbed him in the side. "If they don't want to come in here, they don't have to."

"I'm just playing around," he whispered with an evil grin, "Okay, I'll stop, but only after I get one last stab at them. Hey, chickens—BUK-buk-buk-buk-BUK—whatcha wait'n for?"

Exasperated, Elise shot an angry look at Paige. "That's it! Paige, come on, let's stuff his words right down that little chicken beak of his!" Together, they stomped up beside them. "See, we're not chickens," Elise barked at Jim, "so shut your big trap! We're not afraid—"

CRASH! BOOM! The opening slammed shut, sealing them inside. Frantically, they clawed at the stone wall, but it was no use—they were trapped.

Chapter Eleven

Labyrinth

Only a foot of stone lay between them and freedom, but it might as well have been a mile's worth. Desperately, the boys threw their weight against the wall, hitting the ground with a thud.

"It's no use," Preston said, "it won't budge!"

Crawling on all fours, Jim groped his way back to the granite barrier. "Oh, man, this is bad. I can't see my hand in front of my nose."

All at once, an eerie green glow filled the passage as Paige gazed down at them and frowned. "Something told me I should bring this," she said, holding her Laurelean Bloom out in front of her. "Maybe it might bring us luck."

"It kinda already has," Preston said mindfully. "At least we're not twiddling our thumbs in the dark."

Paige forced out a smile as Elise stared bleakly into Preston's eyes. "What are we going to do? What if they can't find us?"

"Elise, don't worry, it'll be okay," he said, getting to his feet. "Someone's bound to come looking for us soon."

Jim nodded and slid along the wall, crossing his legs as he leaned against it. "Geez, why couldn't I have been a psychic instead of a telepath? At least then I could have seen this coming."

With a smirk, Preston rubbed his hand against the stone. "I still don't get it. Why would they need a tunnel down here?"

"If you're asking me, I really don't care," Jim said dryly. "I'm not planning on making a return visit, so what difference does it make?" Getting up, he scowled at Preston and Paige. "Uh, but now that I think of it, since you guys are *mighty* crescents and all, shouldn't you be able to *blast* a big hole in the wall and get us out of here?"

"Oh, I bet you think that's really funny, don't you?" Paige asked, getting in his face. "Well, big mouth, do you see any of us laughing?"

"Hey, quit it!" Preston said, pointing a finger at Jim. "If you haven't noticed, we're still kinda stuck in here. But just so you know, if we could have done something, we would have done it by now."

Outnumbered, Jim sulked as Paige continued to glare at him. Sighing, Preston peered at his watch, then put an ear to the wall. "Uh, it's after nine o'clock," he said, glancing at his brooding roommate. "They've gotta be wondering where we're at. So, hopefully, we won't need any *super powers* to get out of here."

"It's been over an hour and nobody's come for us," Jim whined pessimistically. "I hate to say this, but things aren't looking so good right now."

Rolling his eyes, Preston could only think of two things—getting out of there and gluing Jim's mouth shut. After stomaching an hour of his non-stop complaining, it had begun to feel like ancient water torture, with every word a drop smacking them on their foreheads. "I can't figure this out—I've been trying to make *something* happen, but I can't even get a puny green spark," Preston said as he gazed at the ceiling, and then at Jim. "Hey, I just thought of something. Do you think you can do whatever-it-is you do to see if anyone's searching for us?"

Jim shrugged as he put his hand against the wall, then grumbled when he pulled it away. "I don't know—this rotten tunnel's messing things up for me. Oh, what am I saying, I'd probably get struck by lightning if I said I was any good at this."

Frustrated, Preston shook his head as he mulled over their dismal choices. "Nobody knows we're in here, you know that, don't you?" Pointing down the passage, he stared grimly at them. "I think our only chance of getting out is that way. So let's take a vote, okay?" Reluctantly, they all nodded. "Uh, who thinks we should go?" he asked, putting his hand in the air. One by one, the others raised their hands. "All right, I guess we walk." Groaning, Preston struggled to his feet, then helped the girls up. "We'd better wish ourselves luck, we'll need it."

As they walked, Elise clung to Preston like a second shadow. *Why did I have to act like a dumb little school girl back in the basement? I'm so stupid. I should have told him how I felt.* In truth, she'd always considered herself bullet-proof to boys and the dumb games they played. One after another, a parade of them had come her way, and still, she'd easily brushed them off. *But Preston,* she thought, *whenever he's around, I'm a complete mess, and I don't know why.*

"Uh, I don't want to be a crybaby, but I'm getting tired...and really thirsty," Elise whimpered. At that moment, everyone slowed to a crawl as if they'd had the same idea in mind all along.

"How long have we been walking?" Paige asked. "It feels like forever."

Blurry-eyed, Preston squinted at his watch as he stopped to shift his weight from one foot to the other. "About two hours. Uh, maybe we should stop and rest here for awhile." With a collective sigh of relief, they dropped to the ground and let out a pathetic moan.

"Boy, I'm starting to think we should have stayed by the basement," Jim said, looking half dead to the world. "I just don't know if leaving that spot was such a good idea anymore."

"Yeah, well, anyway, we'd better try to get some sleep," Preston said, "who knows when we'll get another chance."

The girls nodded as Jim tried to find a comfortable spot. Grumbling, he scowled as he sat back up and stared at Preston. "You know, it's times like this that I appreciate our bunks at school," he said, resting his head against the wall, "but only by a little bit, because they still feel almost as hard as this rock floor."

Trying not to laugh, Elise leaned up against Preston as Paige slipped the Laurelean Bloom into his hand and closed her eyes. Slowly, Preston rolled the luminous stone in his palm, and then, without a word, he dozed off.

SNAP! CLANG! The sounds echoed off the walls of the passage, rattling through Preston's brain. "What...huh...wha...? The stone?" he shouted, brushing his hands across the floor. "I can't see! No! I couldn't have dropped it! This has to be a dream, it's got to be!

Wake up!"

Crawling on all fours, he groped through the darkness. "Guys, get up, I can't find the stone," he cried. "Help me!" Silence – not a sound. "Where are you? What's happening?" Wildly, he thrashed his arms about, slamming into the wall as he tumbled forward. *Which way – which way should I go?*

CRACK! BANG! "Who's there?" Preston yelled. "Answer me!" *Wait, something's up there – a light!* "Hey, where'd it go?"

Struggling up the rise, he climbed to where the flash went off, then stumbled and flew end-over-end. THUMP! Skidding to a stop, he gasped as he stared up at the glowing eyes of a skeleton. As he moved closer, beams of fiery light shot from the sockets, casting a ghostly amber hue across the walls. Kneeling over the grimacing corpse, he looked over its tattered clothing.

"Two green braids? Just like my uniform. And what's it got in its hand?" Cringing, Preston reached out to grab it, holding his breath as he came within inches of touching the dead hand. "Geez, like I really want to do this," he said squeamishly. "Ah…oh, gross." One finger at a time, he pried open the bony fist, when all at once, it fell apart, releasing its possession. "A map? I don't get it." Folding it in half, he shoved it into his coat and smirked at his gruesome companion.

"So, what now? Oh, wait, cat got your tongue?" *And your nose, ears, and everything else,* he quipped. "You hiding anything else? A candy bar or a soda would be nice." Carefully, Preston slipped his hand into the skeleton's pockets, pulling out an assortment of candy wrappers and trash. "At least you had good taste," he said, studying each one, "these are my favorites, especially this one." Putting the clothes back into place, he shook his head. "What were you doing here? Who the heck are you?"

In answer, the amber glow faded to black. "No! That's not fair! You can't do this!" Sliding against the wall, Preston sat there amid the gloom. Suddenly, the skull's sockets exploded into two brilliant orbs, one shimmering in indigo blue and the other in emerald green. Dropping the wrappers, he scrambled backwards as hundreds of green and blue tendrils encircled the corpse. In a matter of seconds, skin swam over the skeleton as it shaped itself into a lifeless copy of Preston!

Terrified, he stared at his dead double in disbelief. "No, it's a trick, that can't be me!"

From the depths of the tunnel, an answer came in the form of a whisper. "A deception? No. It is your future—if events remain on their present course," the voice said impassively. "*She* desires your death beyond all her earthly needs and is bent on achieving it at all costs, that is, if you cannot be swayed."

"But, why me?" Preston shouted. "What did I do?"

"Why?" the voice replied. "It is but a simple twist of fate, a mere plunge in the genetics pool, nothing more, nothing less."

Tears streamed down Preston's face as the anger welled up inside him. "So that's it? What about Paige, what's going to happen to her?"

"The path of future events remains in motion. The key—you *both* must find it within yourselves. *She* seeks what you seek. Look beyond the Dark Valley, to the mountain twins. There, the answer lies—in the darkness—"

As the voice trailed off, Preston's dead twin quivered as its skin dissolved away, leaving the skeleton smiling up at him. Soon, the luminous orbs faded as well, and again, darkness prevailed. "Fine—I like the dark!" Struggling to his feet, Preston stumbled through the gloom as he moved farther into the maze.

Hitting the brakes, he put his hands to the wall. *Something's wrong.* All at once, a rumbling quake jolted the passage, showering him with chucks of rock as he bolted blindly down the trail. Suddenly, the floor gave way, sending him spiraling downward. Flailing his arms, he tried to grab hold, and then, with a thunderous crash, he hit bottom!

In blood-curdling stereo, Paige and Preston screamed as they sprang from a dead sleep. Caught in the crossfire, Jim and Elise shot up in a stupor, ending up on their rear ends as they collided head-on.

"Wha…where, huh?" Jim asked, catching his breath. "What happened?"

As his head spun, Preston's eyes darted around the tunnel, and then to his hand. In his palm, the stone shined. "Uh, I must've had a nightmare," he said as Paige stared uneasily at him.

"Me too," she said, squinting at Jim and Elise. "Sorry."

Jim rocked his head from side to side and scowled. "That figures, just when I was having a great dream, you guys go and mess it up."

"So what should we do now?" Paige asked halfheartedly. "I really don't think I can go back to sleep."

Preston closed an eye and gazed at his watch, trying to focus on the glowing numbers. "Crud, it's four in the morning!" Wincing, he forced out a smile, then got up and tried to rub the pins and needles from his legs. "Uh, we might as well get going."

Wearily, they began walking down the bleak path as Jim wrinkled his nose at Preston. "So, what was your dream about? It sounded like a real whopper."

Preston began rattling off the details, and as he neared the climax of his story, he performed the final act, moving his hands as he walked. "—so, right after that, the *whole* place started shaking and I ran for the hills. Then, WOOSH! I fell into a big, black pit." Slipping his hands into his jacket, Preston sputtered as he stopped dead in his tracks. Petrified, he held out a tattered piece of old parchment as their mouths gaped open.

"Preston?" Paige asked as she squeezed in for a better view. "That can't be the map, can it?"

His eyes narrowed as he unfolded it. "No, it was just a nightmare, it can't be real."

A look of dread washed over Paige's face as she stepped back and searched her own pockets. Turning pale, she froze and gawked at Preston. "In my dream, I found a piece too." Wide-eyed, she handed Preston another ragged piece of the map.

"Oh, man, this can't be good," Jim groaned. "Don't we have enough problems?"

"Yeah, lots of them," Preston said with a frown. Holding the pieces out in front of him, he stared intently at Paige. "*She's* after these, you know that don't you? I'm almost sure of it."

"She?" Jim asked incredulously. "Ah, clue me in, will ya? Who are you talking about?"

Taking a deep breath, Preston gave them a quick blow-by-blow account of what he and Paige had known all along. "—so this glowing-glob-of-goo is still after us. And if we don't find what *She's* looking for before *She* does, we're all going to be in a world of hurt."

Instantly, Jim went red as he clutched his strawberry hair in his hands. "Going to be? We're already in a world of hurt," he countered, throwing his arms in the air, "and unless you know a way out, it isn't gonna matter what your glob lady's going to do to us if we're all rotting down here."

"What? You just don't get it, do you?" Preston yelled. "If *She's* waiting up there, we'll be in more trouble than you ever thought. I'm telling you, *She'll* mow through anyone who gets in her way." Warily, he peered down the dark pathway. "Honestly, I'm not sure what to do, but I'm beginning to think Jim's right. We've got to find a way out soon—the sooner, the better."

Chapter Twelve

The Lost

"Holy crud, I can't believe it," Jim exclaimed, shaking his head, "this psycho glob-lady tosses a freight train at you and Paige, and you're still breathing, that's un-freaking-believable." With a smirk, he gawked at Paige and whistled. "Boy, I guess I'd better watch what I say around you—a whole train—POOF! Right through everything! Oh, man, only the best of the *flakes* can do that." In a flash, another thought popped into his mind. "You know, I think I'm gonna ask *Santa* if I can be a crescent," he said as he pounded his chest, "then I would be *invincible!*" Paige rolled her eyes as Jim elbowed Preston in the side. "What a waste, you guys have all these great bells and whistles, but you don't know how to turn them on. Now, you've got to admit that's pretty hilarious."

Scoffing at Jim's humor, Preston shot back. "Yeah—yeah,

sure. We might not be able to turn them on, but if you could, you'd have a permanent seat in detention."

Paige and Elise giggled as Jim stuck his tongue out at them. "So you think that's funny, huh? Well, good, at least you've got something to laugh about in here. I'm glad I could help."

Giving Jim a sympathetic smile, Preston patted him on the back. "Hey, I'm joking. Besides, you're right, it is sort of a waste."

"Okay, whatever, but we better get out of here soon, because my tongue's gonna shrivel up and die," he said, letting it flop out of his mouth. "See, it looks like chalk and tastes like it too. Why is there never a soda machine around when you need one?"

As they heard the word soda, they all groaned and slowed to a miserable crawl. "Why'd you have to say that?" Paige grumbled and wet her lips. "I almost forget how thirsty I was."

Mouthing the word sorry, Jim dropped his head, and walked a few steps ahead as Elise gazed anxiously at Preston. "Preston…uh, back in the basement," she said softly. "When you said those things—you know, that you liked me."

Preston tensed up as he shook his head, trying to lessen the blow of what he knew was coming next. "Elise, it's all right. I'm sorry I got all mushy and stuff. Honestly, I don't blame you for thinking I'm an idiot, I bet I have the word stamped across my forehead."

"Preston, I don't think that at all. I just didn't want to say something stupid, but I guess I messed things up instead."

Wrinkling his nose, he stared curiously at her. "Messed things up? I don't get it—messed what up?"

"Oh, I can't say it," she said, and then blurted out the first thing that came to mind. "I think I love you—no, I really do!" As if they'd all been the victims of an ambush, everyone froze in place, their eyes focused on Elise. "I mean I…uh…oh, I told you I'd sound stupid."

Hit by a truckload of bricks in the shape of an eleven year-old girl, Preston put his hands to his face and looked at her through his fingers. *Girls – I swear I'm never going to figure them out, not a chance.*

"Preston?" Elise snapped. "Say something!"

"Elise, come on, I'm glad you told me." Leaning forward, he whispered into her ear. "I'm crazy about you. Geez, I think about you all the time." Kissing her on the cheek, he took her hand, and they all continued down the path. Slowly, the hours passed, smothering any hope they had of finding a way out.

"I don't know if I can do this anymore," Elise moaned, "I'm so tired."

Coming to a grinding stop, they slid down against the wall like limp dolls. In the murky light, Preston squinted at his watch. "It's almost eight in the morning and we still haven't found a way out." Angrily, he pounded his fist against the floor, then got to his feet and walked farther ahead. "We've tried everything—I don't know what else to do."

"Maybe we should go back," Paige suggested, "at least it's bett—"

"Go back?" Jim shouted, cutting her off. "Oh, yeah, what a great idea! We've been in this hamster trail for over ten hours—it'll take us forever to get back there, if we get there at all!"

Exasperated, Paige glared at him as Preston waved the glowing bloom at them. "Hey, you guys, be quiet," he said under his breath, "I hear something." Turning in his direction, they clammed up as he disappeared around the bend. Seconds later, he came running back, looking as if he'd won the lottery. "It's water—up that way!"

Scrambling to their feet, they sped through the tunnel, slamming into one another as the passage spilled out into a vast underground grotto.

Brimming with huge stalactites which hung from the ceiling and hundreds of enormous stalagmites that shot upwards from the cave floor, the cavern seemed like a portal to a prehistoric past long since lost.

"It's beautiful," Paige exclaimed as the cavern fluoresced in the bloom's light. Above them, in the distance, twin waterfalls sprang from thin air, emptying into a large black lagoon. At the far end, hot springs bubbled up to the surface, sending plumes of steam into the air.

Hopping down to the path below, they dropped to their knees at the water's edge in a race to find out who would get their fill first. Getting to his feet, Preston glanced around the cavern. "Uh, at least it's warm in here—there's lots of water, too."

Jim gulped down another mouthful and gurgled something incoherent as he grinned at him. "—ummm, now, if you could come up with a fast food restaurant, I'd promise to not cause you any more problems in class—ever, I swear."

Rolling his eyes, Preston sighed as he stared at the girls. "We might want to stay here and get some sleep before we start again. As much as I hate to say it, this might be the only water we see for awhile." Searching for a good spot to lie down, he settled for one near the hot springs, then listened to the bubbles pop quietly on the water's surface. A few feet away, Paige and Elise lay gazing up at the rainbow of colors. One by one, they called out each color they saw, while Jim whistled softly to himself—then, with hardly a sound, they drifted off to sleep.

Within the endless winding labyrinth of tunnels, time held no dominion over the wicked creatures that lurked in the darkness. Driven underground centuries ago, her dark followers rotted there, decaying into a twisted and evil army as they waited for the day *She* would return.

Once, the dark ones walked the planet as Outlanders, following the same footpaths that all men traveled. Simple pleasures, such as the first light of dawn and the serenity of nightfall captivated them, for the essence of nature and their very existence had become one. But, as time passed, questions about who they were and why they were different than others began to plague their dreams. It was at this grave crossroads that *She* came upon them.

Exhibiting abilities that far outshined their own, her knowledge of nature and its bond with the Outlanders astounded them. Self-assured, *She* promised answers to all their questions, and willingly, they followed her. Hiding behind a cloak of friendship, *She* exploited their desires, spreading her cancerous thoughts throughout their growing numbers, until ultimately, their fate was sealed. Blinded by greed and a hunger for power, they allowed themselves to become pawns in her wicked plans, gladly selling their souls for promises of immortality and riches. One by one, *She* consumed them, making them slaves to their own unquenchable desires.

Now, the memories of their days in the sun had long since faded into the shadowy recesses of their minds. The black gloom of the underground had replaced day and night, and the miles of forsaken passageways had become their home. A soulless dark army, they had become eternally bound to her as they waited to exact their bitter revenge on those who drove their mistress from the Emerald Mountains.

Dark-shifters—like spiders on a web, the three of them crept through the winding labyrinth. As they stalked their prey, only the faint glow of their indigo eyes warned of their silent approach.

In the air, something had changed. A sound? A scent? Abandoning human form, they hid in the dark, morphing into three massive black panthers. Slowly, they raised their heads and inched closer. Focusing on the tunnel opening ahead, they stopped and stood motionless as the leader let out a rumbling snarl. Before them, a faint greenish haze cut through the void, revealing what had wandered into their domain—four children lying near the water's edge.

Chapter Thirteen

Melee

I can't sleep, Paige thought, *and my back hurts. I wish Jim would stop snoring. Oh my gosh, he's even annoying when he sleeps.* With a deep sigh, she stared up at the ceiling. *The great outdoors – yuck.* Every time her mom and dad brought up the subject of camping, she always used the same three reasons for not wanting to go. *Bugs. Bears.* And the number one reason—*no restrooms.* Sure, it was supposed to be fun or at least that's what they'd told her, but if lying on this rock was anything like it, she was glad she'd always said no.

This is awful – I'm never going to find a comfortable position. Sitting up, she plucked the bloom from Preston's hand and waved it around the grotto as she tried to put names to the different rock formations. One resembled a giraffe and another looked like an upside down hippo.

Hey, what's that? Something's moving over there. Craning her neck, she peered towards the shadows. *Yeah, there it is again.* Slowly, her eyes focused on the dark shape as it separated and spread out in three directions. Wide-eyed, she slid backwards as she realized what they were—three huge black cats!

"Preston, wake up!" Paige yelled. "PRESTON!"

In a gruesome blur, the cats morphed into human form in mid-air, landing in front of Jim and Elise. Stretching their arms outward, they shaped them into monstrous thrashing tentacles, then snatched Jim and Elise off the ground. Quickly, the two shifters carried them screaming into the tunnel as their leader, still in feline form, came within striking distance of Preston and Paige. Snarling, the sleek cat transformed into a hissing serpent, growing long snaking limbs that snapped and cracked as they hit rock. With a whipping motion, it snared Preston and Paige by the legs, dragging them towards it.

"Let go of me! Leave me alone!" Paige cried. "Preston, help me!"

Clawing at the ground, Preston used every ounce of his strength as he kicked at the serpent's limb wrapped around his right leg. WOOSH! The dark-shifter pulled them up and stared at them as they dangled upside down. In a sickening, watery cascade, its head melted away to reveal the face of a dark, strikingly beautiful woman. "Young ones, why do you struggle so?" she said woefully. "Like sand through your hands, it is futile." Swinging around, she carried them through the winding maze. Suddenly, the passage went dark as Paige dropped the bloom and started to sob.

"Paige, don't cry," Preston said, "we'll get out of this, I

swear." Powerless, he felt the anger well up inside him as his mind spun wildly out of control. "Why are you doing this to us?" Grabbing at air, he thrashed about. "Let us go, we didn't do anything!" Coldly, the woman ignored him and raced through the blackness as he listened in horror to Jim and Elise's cries for help from deep within the tunnel.

"Elise!" Preston shouted. "Where are you?" No answer. "Elise? Jim?" Nothing. "What are they doing to them?" Drowning in desperation, he closed his eyes as his blood began to boil. *I've got to do something before it's too late, I have to!* While his mind raced, his body started to quiver and convulse as the aura around him erupted in a blinding shower of fireworks. Knocked off balance, the woman released her grip and dropped them as she staggered backward.

Hitting the ground, Preston scrambled to his feet, then grabbed Paige and ran the other direction as beams of light danced off the walls. Frantic, he looked back only to see two of the dark-shifters, once again in cat form, charging toward them. Grinding to a stop, he spun around and glared at them as Paige watched in absolute horror. "Preston? What are you doing? They're coming!"

In the center of the path, Preston stood his ground as a blaze of emerald and indigo flames engulfed him. A split second later, the cats lunged, tackling him to the ground. "Preston!" Paige screamed, backpedaling away. "Get off of him!"

Without warning, his body exploded into hundreds of burning embers, each one morphing into a fiery scorpion. Swarming the two dark-shifters, they drove their stingers into them in rapid succession. Dealt the final blow, one fell to the ground dead, its body melting away to bones.

In a wild frenzy, the remaining cat jerked and thrashed on the ground, transforming into a horde of giant wasps as it broke away from Preston's deadly attack. Swiftly, the wasps escaped into the passage as the scorpions shifted into hundreds of shimmering bats and took flight in pursuit. Spiraling through the tunnel, the flailing mass of wasps and bats battled each other as Paige ran after them. Soon, the fight spilled out into another cavern, illuminating the walls in an eerie aqua-marine glow as the mid-air melee continued.

"Preston—stop!" Paige cried as she peeked out of the opening. "Please!"

Hearing Paige's pleas, the wasps broke off their attack and swarmed her. Instantly, the bats countered their move and encircled Paige, protecting her as the insects veered away. Swirling inward, the wasps vanished, leaving only the woman standing in the cavern's center. "You! You killed my brother!" she thundered, her eyes blazing in indigo. "I promise, you will soon regret that!"

In answer, the bats scattered and formed into a blazing twister from which Preston emerged. Aflame, he glared at her as Paige hid behind him. "You're off your rocker lady—you started this, not me!"

Furious, she took a few steps toward Preston as Jim came running in from the passageway behind her. "Hey, Preston, I've—" he shouted as the woman sneered at him. "Oh, crud, talk about being in the wrong place at the wrong time."

Flanked by the two boys, she stared indifferently at Jim and turned back to Preston. "Boy, we are eternal—yet, you have slain my brother," she said mournfully. "Who—and what are you?"

"I'm just a kid who's having a really bad day, and you're not making it any better!"

"Boy! You have but a mere inkling of how dire your situation truly is!" As the woman moved in on Preston and Paige, Jim tried to slide past her, then slammed on the brakes as she blocked his way.

"Preston, watch out," he yelled, "she's going to—"

Whipping her arm around, she knocked Jim up against the wall, and swung back in their direction. "You little fools! You are going to wish you had never come down here!" In the blink of an eye, she rose upward to the ceiling, growing into a monstrous winged beast. Turning scaly and gray, she sprouted razor sharp claws as her head stretched and separated into two. Swiftly, she dropped down on all fours and charged at them, her talons scratching against the rock floor as she closed in. Sucking back two huge mouthfuls of air, she reared up onto her hind legs and spewed a rain of blue fire at them.

In a panic, they ran for cover, darting through the cave opening as the wall of flame surged towards them. Running at a full tilt, Preston pulled Paige behind him until she fell to her knees, gasping for air. "Preston, I can't run anymore, I can't breathe."

He stared down the length of the passageway, then threw her a grim look. "Paige, she's trying to burn us alive! Come on, we've got to keep moving!" Grabbing her hand, he spurred her along as he raced down the path, and again, she fell and started to sob. "I…I'm sorry, I shouldn't have gone so fast." Up the straight-away, he focused on the end of the tunnel. In the distance, subtle shades of blue flickered off the walls, then gave way as the raging inferno came rolling at them.

"Paige! Stay close to me," Preston shouted, shielding her. Placing his hands out in front of him, he closed his eyes as bolts of indigo and emerald current shot from his hands, generating a pulsing screen around them. At that instant, the coursing wave of fire smashed into them with the force of a wrecking ball as Paige screamed in terror.

Desperately, Preston fought to hold the blaze at bay, digging his feet into the ground as he drove the firestorm away from them.

The passage shook violently as the hellfire reversed course, gaining speed as it roared back towards its source.

Acting as if her attack had succeeded, the two-headed monstrosity turned on Jim as he ducked into a nearby tunnel. Lumbering his direction, she prepared to unleash another rain of fire, when the cavern began to shake down to its foundation. Spinning around, she was struck by her own fiery weapon and sent flying backwards as the flames exploded from the opening.

With Paige in tow, Preston ran into the cavern, hands ablaze in aqua-blue, and glared at the smoldering dark-shifter. "Why? We didn't do anything to you—it didn't have to be this way."

Discarding her monstrous guise, the woman returned to human form, and stared scornfully at Preston, spitting blood as she spoke. "Boy. Your ignorance—it spites me. You believe you have won, but truly, it is folly. Auric, my brother, they will pay a heavy price for what they have done—that, I promise you." Letting out a deafening shriek, she transformed into a tangled mass of sewer rats and scattered.

Completely spent, Paige and Preston stood there speechless as Jim jumped down from his hiding place and cringed. "Yikes, I hate rats—totally disgusting."

Preston scowled at him. "Jim, where's Elise? What happened to her?"

"I don't know, it was dark in there," he said, scratching his head. "All I remember is getting dumped on my head when that shifting whatever-he-was took off running. Geez, I'm not even sure how I got here."

Angrily, Preston kicked at the dirt floor. "We've got to find her—she's alone in there somewhere." Wiggling his glowing fingers near his face, he gazed at the blue and green flames, then climbed up into the passage and waved down at them. "Come on, let's go." Helping them up, he walked a few steps inside, using his hands to light the way. "From now on, we have to be careful, okay?"

Paige and Jim gave him a quick nod, then started moving forward. Step by step, they retraced Jim's footsteps, but soon faced another stomach-turning fork in the path. Amid the gloom, they stared at each other as Jim shuffled nervously in place. "Uh, I don't remember this at all," he moaned, drumming his fist against his forehead.

Kneeling down in front of the two tunnels, Preston ran his hand over the ground as he checked for tracks. "I think this is the way," he said, pointing to the left as they squirmed in place. "Come on, we've got to hurry."

"Preston, I'm getting worried," Paige said, glancing behind them. "Maybe we should go back and try the other way."

Frowning, he pinched the bridge of his nose and sighed. "Yeah, I've been thinking the same thing for a while, but I've got to sit down for a minute, my legs are killing me." In record time, they slid to the ground, acting about as festive as a party of zombies, only zombies seemed a whole lot livelier. Leaning against the wall, Preston closed his eyes. "I really thought we were going the right way—what a waste of time." He squinted at his watch and let out a loud groan as he shook it. "I can't stand it—it's busted!" In anger, he threw it into the shadows, then got to his feet and started pacing. "Okay—fine, I guess we go back."

Halfheartedly, they got up and began to walk in the direction they came, when the sound of footsteps echoed behind them. "Preston, is it them?" Paige whispered. "Are they back?"

Squeezing her hand, he brought his finger to his lips. "Shhh, I'm not sure." Gathering his courage, he raised his flaming hands and took a few steps forward. "Hey! Who's in there?"

Bit by bit, the sounds inched closer, when finally, an answer came. "It…it's me…Elise." Gingerly, she limped into the light and fell to her knees.

"Elise!" Preston yelled as he ran to her side. "No!"

Bruised and bleeding, she stared numbly at them as a feeling of gloom rolled in once more. Dropping to the floor, Preston put his jacket over her and guided her next to him. "We can't leave until she feels a little better. You guys should try to get some sleep, I'll keep watch."

While the others slept, Preston gazed curiously at his right hand, still aglow in indigo. Wrinkling his nose, he tried to *force* some sort of change, but the flames remained constant. *Weird, why's the fire in two different colors? And why can't I turn it off?* He shook off the thought as Elise moaned. "Elise? It's me—Preston."

Snapping upright, her eyes darted around the tunnel, ending up on Preston. "Wha…what happened?" After giving the shortest version possible, he slipped his hand into hers and sat quietly with her, letting the minutes pass.

"Preston," she said, staring into the black void. "Uh, I'm really not sure if I imagined it, but I think I saw a way out when that thing let go of me."

"What?" he asked as his mouth dropped open. "Are you sure?"

"Yes, I think so—I wanted to look, but I could hear him running back and forth. Preston, I'm sure I can find it again."

Numb from head to toe, his mind began to race. "Paige! Jim!"

he shouted, prodding them. "Get up! Elise says she saw a way out of here!" Jolted awake, they scrambled to their feet, then anxiously followed Elise's lead as the chatter of their questions ricocheted off the walls.

"Is it true?"

"Are you sure?"

"Where?"

"How far?"

Recklessly, they tripped and hobbled through the winding labyrinth, only to come upon a dead end. "Look! Up there!" Preston yelled as he pointed to a small pizza-sized hole. "Daylight!" One by one, they climbed out and gazed out over a beautiful green valley.

Chapter Fourteen

The Patchwork Parchment

"No Mom, you don't have to come up here," Preston said as Paige waved her hands to get his attention, "we're okay—yeah, I'm sure. Oh...uh, Paige really wants to talk to you."

Rolling his eyes as he handed her the phone, he leaned back in his seat and blew out a breath. Even after three days, the effects of a day-and-a-half spent underground lingered. It wasn't until yesterday in the afternoon that they'd finally dragged themselves out of bed and into the lounge. But across campus, rumors were spreading at a breakneck speed, and just as fast, their status as the new kids at school turned to overnight celebrity.

"Why do we have to talk to Miss *high-and-mighty* Lumenayre

today?" Jim asked as they headed to the rec hall. "I bet she's trying to mess up my vacation."

"Vacation? Maybe you haven't noticed, but we're up to our ears in trouble," Preston exclaimed, kicking the gravel as he walked. "Geez, she'll probably punt us out the front door the minute she sees us."

With a collective sigh, they walked up over the grassy rise only to find Paige and Elise waiting by the hall. "Hey, guess what," Jim said, smirking at them. "I think we've got the place all to ourselves." Walking inside, Jim clapped his hands together and grinned from ear to ear. "So, where to first, the arcade or the gaming center—or do you want to play some laser tag upstairs?" After a quick vote, the first floor won. Scattering, they spent a good two hours playing before meeting up at the snack bar.

"Now, this is styling," Jim announced as he took a gulp of his soda. "We get to do anything we want while everyone else has to sit in class. Come on, you gotta admit this is great." Drawing in a breath, he leaned back and put his feet on the table. "You know, if this is what we get for being in trouble, we've definitely got to do it again."

All of a sudden, a voice boomed from the wall speaker. "Mr. Richardson, get your feet off the table—now! I'm not going to say it again."

Startled, Jim dropped his legs and glanced around the room. "It's Miss busy-body-Becca—how she ever became an overseer boggles my mind. She's just a snitch like Aubree, only bigger," he said, scowling at Paige. "She's got it out for me—all because of that food fight last September." They rolled their eyes at him as he rushed to his own defense. "Hey, I didn't start it, I only helped finish it." Finding the nearest surveillance camera, he stuck his tongue out at it.

"Anyway, that's old news. So, what should we do now?"

Reaching into his back pocket, Preston laid the two map pieces on the table. "I think we need to figure these out," he said, flipping them over and shifting them around. "Huh? Wait a minute—they don't fit. Something's missing." Shaking his head, he stared up at the ceiling. "Great, can we get any more unlucky? We've only got half a map."

Carefully, Elise slid the pieces over and studied them for a second. "Ummm, why don't we ask Mr. Beadle when we see him today?" she suggested. "I mean, it couldn't hurt to ask, could it?"

Preston shrugged as he looked at Jim and Paige. "Sure, why not—he knows this place way better than we do."

Lunch came to a grinding halt after another battle between Aubree and Jim, and soon, the four kids found themselves gazing up at the doors of Manderlane Hall. Making a face, Preston put his hands against them. "There's gotta be a trick to opening these things, but I can't figure it out," he said, waving a hand in front of them. "See, they won't budge."

"Preston, maybe you should use the intercom," Paige said as he scoffed at her, "it might be easier."

Narrowing his eyes, he turned his nose up at her as he continued to fan the doorway. "Easier—sure, but where's the fun in that? Besides, I know what I'm doing."

"Yeah, uh-huh, but maybe you're not doing it right?"

Preston's mouth fell open. "Not doing it right? Okay, maybe you can show me the *right* way to do it."

Sighing, Paige stepped around Preston and held her breath. After a quick flick of her wrist, she ran her hand across the center of the doors, and walked away in a huff.

"There, I told you so—nothing happened," he shouted gleefully. "See, I just proved you don't know everything." Gloating, he hopped down the stairs, then grimaced as the doors groaned and flew open with a rumbling thud. Victorious, Paige grabbed Elise by the arm and paraded past them.

"Hey, how'd she do that?" Jim asked. "She didn't even break a sweat."

Stone-faced, Preston shook his head as he watched the girls walk inside, then grabbed Jim and ran for the doors, slipping in just before they slammed shut. Standing a few feet away from them, Paige smirked at Preston as he closed an eye and scratched the side of his head. "Okay, you were right—satisfied?"

Giggling, Paige gave him a coy smile. "I tried to tell you," she said, shaking her head at him as he and Jim followed them grudgingly, "but you never listen to me—ever."

As they approached the elevators, Natewick waved to them from one of the sitting areas. "Well, hello to ya, lads and lasses. I'm glad ya all are feeling better, that's very good news indeed. Why don't we retreat to the lift, so we can talk upstairs?" In short order, they piled into the elevator, and minutes later, were in his office. Sitting down next to Elise, Preston gazed around the room which was chocked full of odd knick-knacks and strange ornamental curios. On the far wall, a warm fire burned in a mantled hearth, and close by, a beautifully engraved chess board sat waiting for the next move.

"I first should mention that Vice-Precept Lumenayre will be, I'm sorry to say, a wee bit late," Natewick announced as the cloud of gloom vanished from over their heads. "But this provides us a grand opportunity to talk first, which is probably best."

Picking up an etched glass jar from his desk, he uncorked it and pulled out a shiny cherry-sized berry. Quickly, he popped it into his mouth and offered the open jar to each of them as they looked squeamishly at it. "Oh, not to worry. These are sweet pinderwhortles—from the east slope of Mount Crittendome. They have a wonderful flavor, I promise ya."

Reluctantly, they each put the purple treats into their mouths. "Hey, these aren't bad at all," Jim said enthusiastically as the others rolled them around on their tongues. "Kinda taste like skittles, only better."

"Well, they truly are a very special delight seeing as they only grow one month out of the year," Natewick said, tossing another into his mouth. "And the weather must be perfect or they won't taste even half as good as these." Setting the jar down, he scooped up two small, ruby colored cubes from his desk and started tumbling them in his hand. "So Preston, why don't we begin with ya? Just give me your recollection of the events up to the point that the hill folk found ya. And if any of ya want to add anything, feel free to jump right in."

"Dark-shifters?" he said, going pale. "So, the rumors were factual, they're still among the living." Getting to his feet, he paced behind his desk. "But what's even worse is that they threatened ya, the loathsome fiends."

Stewing, the little man stared up at the ceiling as Preston pulled the parchments from his pocket. "Uh, Mr. Beadle—the map," he said, setting the pieces on the desk, "we thought you should see it."

Slipping on his half moon spectacles, Natewick studied them. Raising his brow, he looked up at Preston and Paige as he tapped a finger against his lips. "Amazing, ya both conjured these up from your slumber at the same moment? In my days, I've never seen anyone actually pull a mental figment into the physical world. Not only is that unusual, but it's also a very difficult thing to do."

Cagily, he continued to eye the parchments as a soft bell tone sounded from out of thin air. "Oh, the vice-precept—all of this has made me lose track of time," he said as Jim and Preston sank in their seats. Flicking his wrist, the door opened on its own and in walked Vice-Precept Lumenayre.

Oh, crud, we're in trouble, Preston worried as he gazed at the cold, stark expression on her face. *Geez, did somebody die or something? She doesn't look very happy to see us at all.*

"Valerian, how are ya?" Natewick said as she took a seat next to him. "I trust ya had a pleasant day."

"I'm well, but the day turned out to be quite hectic to say the least," she said, staring coolly at them. "It seems that the fervor caused by these four hasn't diminished even slightly. So, I'm finding it difficult to get the attention of the average student without bringing up the threat of a hefty *detention*."

Hearing the word, Jim and Preston slid even farther down into their seats as Natewick winked at them and changed the subject. "Oh…ah, I've taken the liberty of discussing this regrettable incident with them. So, there really isn't a need to detain them any longer, that is, if ya haven't any inquiries of your own."

"No, I haven't any questions," she said, flashing an uncharacteristic smile. "But, although I'm relieved that you're all in good spirits, I would like to get things back to normal. So, I'll expect you all in class tomorrow, okay?" Stunned, they nodded as she pointed an ebony finger at Jim. "And Mr. Richardson, since you caused this incident to occur in the first place, it would be in your best interest to focus your full attention on class in the future, do I make myself clear?"

"Yes ma'am," he muttered, timidly looking down at the floor.

"Good, you all may go now," she said. "Enjoy the remainder of your day, but make sure you're prepared for class tomorrow."

Glancing sheepishly at each other, they slid out of their chairs as Natewick held up the map parchments. "Preston, I'll show these to the chancellor and get with ya afterwards. Oh, and missy, this is for ya." Pulling a small emerald green velvet bag from his coat pocket, he grinned at Paige and set it in front of her.

Quickly untying its silk drawstring, she slipped her hand inside, then perked up as the bag started to glow a brilliant green. "Another Laurelean Bloom! It's so beautiful," she exclaimed, slipping its silver chain over her head. "But, I only told you about losing it a few minutes ago."

"Oh...uh, the chancellor mentioned it in passing, so replacing it seemed the right thing to do," he said, staring awkwardly at the vice-precept. "Well, ya'd better go—ya have a grand day."

After leading the kids to the elevator, Natewick and Vice-Precept Lumenayre walked down the hall to the chancellor's office. "A bloom? That's quite a handsome gift for an eleven year old, isn't it?" she asked as the little man dismissed her comment with a wave of his hand. "Natewick, I'm serious—only a handful of stones are known to exist, and you're giving them away as parting gifts."

"Valerian, I don't presume to take issue when considering the chancellor's decisions," he said sternly, "but the fact remains, if they hadn't had the stone in the tunnels, they may never have found their way out from the underground."

"Yes, that was fortunate. Considering the circumstances, I'm astonished by how well they weathered the ordeal. Even so, I have some concerns about Elise Temberly. She doesn't seem to have the same spark I usually see in her. It might be prudent to have a counselor talk to her."

"I think ya may be right," Natewick said, running a hand through his white hair. "See to it, will ya."

As they reached the end of the hall, the chancellor's door revealed itself. Knocking quietly, they stepped inside, and paused. In the shadows, the chancellor sat motionless, encased in a strange greenish fog.

"Mathias?" Natewick said softly, his eyes narrowing.

Mysteriously, the mist faded as Mathias ran a hand over his face and stared at them. "Uh, I apologize—I'm afraid my immediate attention was required elsewhere."

"Oh...uh, well...Valerian and I finished with the children," Natewick said guardedly as they sat down. "They had quite a lot to say indeed." Step by step, he recounted their story, ending by handing him the map pieces.

Studying each parchment front and back, Mathias shook his head in disbelief. "Extraordinary," he said, pulling out a magnifying glass, "the handwriting, I've seen it before." Leaping from his chair, he rifled through the shelves of books around him, taking one from its perch. In quick order, he thumbed through the pages, slamming his finger down on one of them. "There—I thought it wasn't possible, but it's spot on. And you're saying the Brandymire children pulled these from their dreams?" Natewick raised a brow and nodded as Mathias paced behind his huge mahogany desk. "It's all starting to make sense—these two children, there's something more to them than meets the eye. I believe *She's* pursuing them for that very reason."

Gazing into the fire, Valerian cringed at the notion. "But, they're just children, what would *She* want with them?"

"Think about it—their abilities are beyond their years, their only weakness is that they lack the skill to control them. But considering recent events, I fear this latest incident has only made matters worse. Obviously, the rumors of dark dwellers are true, but what troubles me is that we've been caught unaware—this accompanied by her unforeseen return doesn't bode well at all."

Pulling out a sheet of stationary, he laid it on his desk and gave them a grim look. "I'm afraid this situation has spiraled out of control. I think the time has come to call an emergency meeting of the council—before it's too late."

Chapter Fifteen

Demora Hall

Demora Hall stood high atop the rocky cliffs of Mount Crittendome overlooking the conservatory grounds. Named after Damon Raydencrafft's half-sister, it was the oldest structure on campus. For years, he worked tirelessly on the hall's construction until his mysterious disappearance just days before its completion. As a result, the building sat empty for years, slowly becoming the fodder of rumors, until a young vice-precept by the name of Mathias Manderlane rallied for its restoration.

Even now, tales of hidden tombs and haunted spirits were the subject on each and every student's mind as they stared up at the great hall's ominous stone face. But if one could float over the edge of the moss-covered cliffs and cross the grassy expanse, they would see Demora Hall as more of an enduring monument than a ghoulish haunted house.

Natewick paced in front of the Demora Hall's entrance as he awaited the arrival of the regent board members. From the east, their private helicopter approached, and as it set down, three men and a woman stepped out. One after another, they shook the little man's hand, then climbed the giant granite steps leading to the hall's columned portico.

Upon entering the atrium, they glanced around the spacious sunlit lobby leading to the main assembly hall. Emerald beams of light filtered down from the stained glass dome onto the portraits of past chancellors and regents that lined the walls. But among them, one painting stood out from the rest—a haunting portrait of Demora Raydencrafft.

With a menacing gray sky as her backdrop, she gazed down at them, wearing an expression of melancholy that revealed her very soul. Forever young, she stood there, adorned in midnight lace and emerald green satin, eternally lost in the mists of time.

"Demora—she was beautiful," one regent said somberly as the others looked on. "What happened to her was tragic." Shaking his head, he smiled and reached for the door. "Well, enough of this, the session's about to begin, we'd better get inside."

Walking across the crowded floor, the four regents hurried to their seats as they passed a who's who of school officials along the way. All at once, a hush fell over the room as a bell tone sounded, and then Mathias climbed the steps to the podium. "Today, we stand perilously on the edge of an abyss, our worst fears coming to fruition as we speak—" Recounting the sobering events that had plagued the conservatory over the last few months, he ended with the discovery of the underground dwellers. "—if the accounts the children gave are accurate, the impenetrable aura surrounding these creatures could allow them to slip into our ranks completely unnoticed."

Uneasy whispers rolled through the assembly as he raised his hands in the air. When the rumbles subsided, one regent spoke up. "Chancellor, if what you've said is true, what would you propose we do?" she asked. "The conservatory has no militia, and campus security is limited to say the least."

"Yes, you're correct, of course. But there are measures we can take, such as locking down the lower floors of all buildings, and heightening security in areas that are at high risk. It might also be a good idea to install additional security sensors around the perimeter of the campus, and require every student to stay on a buddy system."

Again, more murmurs cut through the air.

"Chancellor Manderlane, this is all well and good, but how does this solve anything?" asked Mordachi Wickvane, dean of the conservatory's high school. "What you propose is just a meager bandage for a much larger problem. A problem, I might add, that's growing as we speak."

Mathias gazed up at the ceiling, then threw a testy look at the dean. "A bandage? Well, yes, it provides only a temporary fix, but recent events may have turned the tide in our favor."

His eyes widening, Dean Wickvane stared skeptically at him. "If you're referring to the Brandymire children, I can hardly imagine what assistance you could expect from them—they're far too young and inexperienced. And even if our situation has indeed taken a turn for the worse, I'm still not about to buy into your *crescent* gibberish—neither will the vice-chancellor when she returns."

Instantly, the crowd erupted in an angry debate as Mathias shook his head. "Enough of this," he shouted as the room went silent.

"We can't let our differences cloud the issues that are confronting us."

From the sidelines, Natewick watched with growing apprehension as the discussion raged on. All of a sudden, a shiver ran down his spine, carrying a dreadful feeling that something evil moved among them.

"Hey Terrin, where's Elise?" Aubree asked, squeezing past her as she tore open a bag of crackers. "It's almost lights out."

Terrin shrugged as she wrinkled her nose. "I thought I saw her in the study hall a few minutes ago—want me to go check?"

Shaking her head, Aubree downed the last of the crackers and grabbed a bottle of water. "No—I'll get her, but keep the lights on, okay?"

Slowly, she walked down the hall and poked her head in each doorway, stopping at the study rooms. "Funny, there's nobody here," she whispered, peering in. PING! CLANG! "Who's there?" No answer. "Elise?" Tiptoeing inside, she felt around for a lamp, when from out of the darkness, a black mass encircled her, dragging her away from the light of the hallway. Desperately, she gasped for air as the shadowy glob smothered her with tree-like limbs that sprouted huge poisonous stingers from their tips. Unable to avoid the twisting barbs, an explosion of pain seared through her as the shape drove them deep into her leg. As she fell limp, it callously tossed her against the wall, where she laid deathly quiet.

The shapeless blob stared down at the lifeless girl, then glided across the floor as it morphed into an exact copy of Elise. With a strange curiosity, it cocked its head to one side, following Aubree's bottle of water as it rolled out the door. Calculating its next move, it closed the study hall door, leaving Aubree alone in the dark as it walked to her sleeping chamber and slipped inside.

Chapter Sixteen

The Carbon Copy Counterfeit

A dream—a sickly sweet dream. Whispers drifting on the murky fog. In the distance, flashes of plum-colored light broke through the mist, and then the voices began to beckon.

"Aubree—Aubree Stemson—come on, girl. It's Precept Grievley." As he spoke, waves of radiant energy flowed from his hands, surrounding the lifeless girl in a violet cocoon. Scurrying out into the hall, he motioned to Pete Jeffries, a tall, sturdy type with short cropped hair as black as coal. "She's in a very bad way. I've tried my best to help her, but as she and I are of the same order, I fear that my efforts have been in vain," he said fretfully as they walked to the entrance. "I'm afraid that Chancellor Manderlane is the only one who can help her now. Is he still at Demora Hall?"

"Yes, I believe so," Pete said, his steely gray eyes staring up at the assembly hall, "the council's scheduled to break at midnight."

"Peter, you need to send someone from your security staff to summon him immediately," the little man whispered as he looked uneasily at the three shell-shocked girls fidgeting by Aubree's door. "Uh, and it might be best if you had the girls escorted back to their chambers as soon as you've finished with them."

Nodding, Pete stepped outside, and minutes later, returned to finish questioning Terrin. While they talked, Paige walked over to Aubree's side. "I'm sorry this happened to you," she said grimly, "I really am." Tears streamed down Paige's face as she took Aubree's hand and held it tight. Suddenly, the room lit up in emerald green as a fiery torrent flowed from the infirmary.

As everyone rushed inside, they found Paige balled up in the corner as Aubree lay shrouded within a chrysalis of dazzling flame. "What have you done, girl?" the precept yelled. "Have you lost your mind?"

"I…I'm sorry—I…I didn't," Paige sputtered, "mean to—" At that moment, an awkward silence filled the air as the emerald veil over Aubree vanished. Letting out a cough, she gasped as she cracked open her eyes.

"Aubree?" the girls shouted in chorus. "You're all right!"

Sitting up, Aubree tried to make quick sense of where she was. "What? Where…where am I?"

Curiously, Pete stared at Paige, raising a brow as he looked down at Aubree. "Miss Stemson, how are you feeling?" he asked as she cleared her throat and managed a weak okay. "I know this seems rather sudden, but it's very important—do you remember anything about what happened to you?"

Rubbing her forehead, Aubree gazed at the phony Elise, who smiled devilishly at her. "Ummm, I remember a big black blob and an awful pain in my—" Quickly, she pulled the blankets from her legs, only to find that her wounds had disappeared. "Oh, I don't know."

"That's fine, don't worry about it right now," Pete said, grinning wryly. "We'll discuss it later." With a wave of his hand, he set the girls loose on Aubree as Mathias and Natewick appeared at the doorway. "Chancellor Manderlane, I apologize for having made you come all this way." Scratching his head, he pointed at Paige. "It seems that Miss Brandymire took it upon herself to *help* Miss Stemson."

"So it appears," Mathias said as the girl's mouths fell open. "Hello ladies, I'm Chancellor Manderlane. Miss Stemson, I'm relieved to see that you're feeling better, you gave us quite a scare."

Awestruck, she sat speechless until Terrin jabbed her in the side. "Owww, Terrin! Uh…ummm, thank you, sir."

He took her hand and squeezed it gently, then turned to Terrin. "So, you're the girl that found Miss Stemson, aren't you?" he asked as she smiled back at him. "Well, she should be glad to have you as a friend, that's for certain." Shifting his gaze to Elise, he offered his hand. "Miss Temberly, am I right? Precept Vraden tells me that you've become quite the Pryttonn player." Still grasping her hand, he grinned at her. "I might set some time aside when the season starts, I'd enjoy seeing you play."

"Ummm, I'm really not sure if I'm even going to try out this season," she said, pulling her hand away. "With everything that's happened, I just don't feel very comfortable doing it."

"Now, you wouldn't want to disappoint your friends, would you? Besides, I'm sure they'd love to see you play, am I right girls?" he asked as they nodded eagerly.

Forced into a corner, she stared woefully at him.

"Ummm...uh, I guess I could try."

"Good, that's the spirit," he said as he turned to Paige and offered his hand. "Miss Brandymire, I had the pleasure of meeting your mother a while back." As their hands touched, their grasp shimmered like fireworks and burst into flames. Letting go of each other, they glanced around the room to find everyone gawking at them.

"Did you see that?" Terrin whispered to Elise, whose fiery eyes remained glued on them. "That was really weird."

Avoiding their stares, Mathias gazed down at his hands and then at Paige. "My dear, I apologize—I'm not all together sure why that happened."

"That's okay, I'm getting used to these things happening," she said with a heavy sigh. "It's not knowing when they'll happen that really scares me."

"Paige, it's basic human nature to feel that way—more often than not our fears come to the forefront when things become too difficult for us to handle—and fear alone can blind even the strongest among us. But, it is in the quality of our character, our very soul if you will, that we find the strength to prevent ourselves from falling victim to it."

Taking her hand, his expression turned serious, his voice solemn. "When I was around your brother's age, I knew a boy a lot like Preston. He had amazing abilities, even though he hid the fact that he doubted himself. One day, he and his sister were out exploring the hills. Somehow, they wandered off too far and wound up near the border of the Dark Valley."

In silence, the girls hung on his words as he gathered his thoughts and continued. "After deciding to turn around, they began the long hike back, when a grymalkon mountaincat caught their scent. Stalking them for some time, it finally showed itself and chased them through the high grass as the boy pulled his sister behind him. Then, in the blink of an eye, she fell, and just as fast, the cat leapt on her, dragging her screaming into the forest. Standing there alone, he froze as the fear inside him smothered all hope of saving her. Now, to this very day, she still haunts his dreams—and each year, he returns to that very spot to remember the girl he couldn't save."

Mathias stared somberly at the thunderstruck girls, then gave Paige a warm smile. "Tonight, you faced your fears, and helped your friend, much like you did at the ball field weeks ago—that's something that boy couldn't do," he said, checking his watch. "Well, I'm afraid it's getting a little late. Pete will see that you get back to your quarters, but before I go, I must say that I've enjoyed meeting all of you."

Outside the medical building, Natewick followed Mathias to the bottom of the steps and glared at him. "Mathias, aren't ya getting a tad too close to them. I mean, telling them that story of all things—it's risky, that's all I'm saying."

With growing frustration, Mathias looked at him out of the corner of his eye. "Natewick, I appreciate your point, but I still can't shake the feeling I've got about these children—everything that's happened is somehow tied to them."

"Be that as it may, don't ya think we have bigger problems facing us—namely, the Stemson girl's attack? It's clear as day that there's a wolf in the fold hiding in our midst—we have to find this fiend before it attacks another student—*that* should be our first priority."

Over the next few days, an air of unrest settled over the campus as news of Aubree's attack spread. As night fell, the lights that dotted the conservatory went dark one by one. Inside chamber 3-17, the four girls slept while the rhythmic ticking of the clock kept pace with Terrin's snoring.

Silently, Elise's counterfeit copy slipped out of bed and stared at the other girls. Cocking her head, the imposter gazed at Paige, keenly studying her as if trying to see something hidden in the sleeping girl's face. Cracking open the door, she slipped through and tiptoed into the library.

Walking up to the fireplace, she shifted into a cloud of insects, and escaped up the chimney. In a blur, they rocketed across the night sky on a collision course with Manderlane Hall. Through a roof top vent, the swarm gained access to Natewick's office and returned to human form. Spinning around, the dark-shifter focused on the desk. As he rifled through it, he grabbed the two ruby colored cubes from the desktop and smashed them against the wall. "Where are they, little man?" he thundered, smashing the trinkets and curios placed throughout the room. "They have to be here!"

Once he'd had his fill, he blazed into the chancellor's office, fixing his eyes on the portrait of Damon Raydencrafft. "You pathetic fool—now, *She* will make you pay for what you've done." Below the painting the gun metal staff lay gleaming in its case. Shattering the glass, he reached in to grab it, and was instantly hit by a blast of emerald plasma. End over end, he flew backwards into the glass display cases, and staggered to his feet. "Curse you!" he screamed, glaring furiously at the staff. "Your crescent tricks won't help you in the end!" Grabbing the edge of the desk, he launched it full force across the room, then exploded into a swirling mass of winged beetles, escaping into the night.

Minutes later, he reemerged from the library fireplace, and morphed effortlessly back into Elise. Sneaking into their sleeping chamber, he slipped into bed, undetected.

Chapter Seventeen

Unmasked

After the break-in at Manderlane Hall, many were happy to see that Pryttonn tryouts had arrived. Like clockwork, the time-tested ritual of preparing the playing fields for competition kicked into full swing. And while experienced players got ready for the second half of the season, wannabes lined up in hope of squeezing into the rapidly filling rosters.

Watching the tryouts from the stands, Preston sandwiched his face in his hands as he gazed up at the aqua blue sky. *I can't believe Precept Vraden won't even let me tryout. Why do I have to take a beginning Pryttonn course first? It's not fair.* He frowned as he glanced around the field. *Where the heck are they? It's already four. Come on, Elise, you'd better hurry up.* Eyeing the Quadro-Pitch machine in the middle of the field, he wrinkled his nose at the mechanical monstrosity. It had a weird funnel scoop on top and four side-mounted spouts loaded with clips of colored balls, and hardly looked like any pitching machine he'd ever seen.

"Okay," he said, muttering to himself, "but what's that snow-cone maker doing on top of it?"

"That snow-cone maker's called a scorner," Aaron answered as he hopped up beside him. "Get your team's ball in there and everyone else is in a world of hurt. That's because it adds up to one humungous score." He chuckled as Preston sat there with his mouth wide open. "See that lip on top of it? Almost every ball that's hit it has just rolled around and dropped off. It's nearly impossible to get a direct hit, but Precept Dryden's done it twice."

Trying to get a better look, they hopped down a couple of rows as Paige and Elise came walking up the aisle. A few steps behind the girls, Wil bounded up the steps and grinned at Preston and Aaron. "Uh, ready or not, we're here. Let's get this party started."

Wil came up to bat first. After a hiss, the Quadro-Pitch sunk into a concrete pit, loading each clip as it rose to a locked position. Three loud pings were followed by the blast of a horn, and WOOSH—it fired four balls at once, and dropped back into the ground.

In one fell swoop, Wil and the other batters grunted as they swung, only to watch Wil's ball rocket up toward the turquoise energy shield surrounding the playing field. Careening off the sparkling dome, it landed in the yellow ring an inch or two shy of the scorner as Wil pounded his bat in frustration. "Hey, Aaron, did you see that?" he shouted, using his hand as a measuring stick. "I missed it by that much."

"Yeah—yeah, you were lucky," Aaron yelled back. "Do that a few more times and maybe I'll change my mind."

After his at-bat, Wil ambled up to them, smiling from ear to ear. "Wow, that was a lot easier than I thought."

"Hey, didn't I tell you it would be a snap?" High-fiving Wil, Aaron elbowed him as he sat down, then poked Elise. "So, it's almost your turn," he said, smirking at her. "You ready?"

With a halfhearted nod, Elise's imposter gave him a blank stare and looked timidly at the pitching machine. "Oh, wait a minute, I've gotta be having a brain hemorrhage," Aaron said, gawking at Preston and Wil, "because you *can't* be trying to back out of this." Gazing down at the field, a devilish grin came to his face. "Anyway, I guess we'll never know, Precept Vraden's calling your name – so you can't back out now."

In a huff, she brushed past him and made her way down to the field as the Quadro-Pitch loaded another set of clips. In rapid succession, the three pings came, followed by the sounding of the horn, and BOOM—like a rocket, the ball zipped past her before she could even take a swing.

Once again, the machine rose up and shot another missile at her, only this time the pitch hit her square in the head, knocking her to the ground. "Elise!" Preston shouted as everyone scrambled down to the field. Coming within arms reach of her, they all froze as her body jerked and shifted into a horrible progression of warped creatures, finally revealing the man beneath.

In one fluid motion, the dark-shifter sprang to his feet, grabbing Preston around the neck. "Stay back!" he yelled, glaring at the crowd. Sprouting a set of clawed wings, he took flight, pulling Preston up with him.

"Preston!" Paige cried, running beneath them as they flew toward the horizon.

Soaring high above the crowd, Preston's mind raced as he

stared down at the people scattering below him. *What am I going to do? We're too high. I'll fall if I try to fight. What the – ?* In stunned silence, his eyes followed a thunderous mass of emerald fire as it roared up towards them. Gathering speed as it ballooned in size, the surging ball of flame pursued them along their path. At last, the fiery hunter hit its prey full on, sending them spiraling downward in a freefall. Seconds later, the dark-shifter crashed and tumbled down the hillside as Paige watched Preston float to safety.

"Preston, I don't know what happened," she said, running up to him, "I was chasing after you and then that thing came out of me."

Surprised to be among the living, Preston sat up and shook the numb feeling from his head. "What...what did you say?" he asked as his expression changed to shock, "You mean, *you* hit us."

"I'm sorry, it just happened by itself, but I couldn't let you fall, and then you didn't. Oh, I guess I must have done that too—somehow."

Getting to his feet, Preston made a face at her, then glared at the bloodied dark-shifter laying crumpled on the ground. "Where's Elise?" he screamed. "I swear, you better tell me or I'll—"

"Or you'll do what, you little fool!"

Preston's hands began to glow as the imposter peered intently at them. "So, you mean to kill me, is that it?" he asked with a cold sneer. "Do as you wish—my death will not bring your friend back—she is lost to you." Jolted by his sudden implication, Preston backed away in tears. "You're crying? So, you are a coward—far too yellow to deal the final blow."

Slowly, he labored to his feet, raising a fist at Preston. "Boy, if you haven't the stomach for it, my final task will be easily accomplished." Lunging forward, his body twisted and contorted into the shape of a panther, then charged at Preston. But as the cat closed in on him, a shimmering turquoise field of energy ensnared it.

"Foul creature—how dare you!" Precept Vraden shouted, tightening her grip on the cat as it fought to break free. "Mark my words—you'll pay dearly for what you've done."

As the crowd watched the cat struggle, Preston gazed mournfully into his sister's eyes. "Paige, what if they've done something to Elise?" he said, glancing at the dark-shifter. "No one even knows where she is—except for him."

Chapter Eighteen

WraithVoordan

Beyond the wastelands of An'nonne Duerre, the bewitched wildwoods of Scrimmhain Forest stretched out for as far as the eye could see. From high above, the ocean of green trees appeared calm, but beneath them another world lay hidden.

In this netherworld, nature blotted out the sun, transforming the forest into a cruel playground for her rising power and influence. And now that the hand of fate had released her from an endless purgatory, *She* returned to reclaim the forest as her own, making its black heart hers once more.

Lying buried in the center of Scrimmhain were the fortress ruins of Wraithvoordan. A shell of its former self, the stronghold had long since fallen victim to time's relentless march. Outside its stone walls, pits of steaming tar bubbled and spewed, their sickening fumes resting heavy on the air. At the entrance, the massive iron gates that once barred entry had fallen to the ground, rusted and broken. A few paces past them, two enormous stone dragons stood guard, each holding a cauldron of indigo flame in their claws. Like giant sentries, they watched over the massive steps that led into the ruins, warning those who dared to venture beyond their gaze to go no farther.

For hundreds of years, no mortal man had dared set foot inside Wraithvoordan's decaying labyrinth of slanting halls and crumbling dead ends—for they led to the very depths of evil that had consumed her soul. But now, within this twisted maze, a mere mortal lived among them. Down a series of dim halls, one could barely make out the faint sound of a girl crying in the shadows.

I want to go home, Elise thought. *I haven't done anything wrong. What do they want from me?* Putting an eye to the crack in the door, she peered down the blue-lit corridor. Against the far wall, a surly guard sat, looking the other direction. "Mister? Please help me—please." No response. "Mister? I'm hungry, can I—?" Irritated, he picked up a stone and threw it against the door without uttering a single word. Jumping backwards, Elise sat down and rocked back and forth, sobbing as she tried desperately to choke back her fears.

Through a maze of murky passageways, a procession of her dark followers weaved their way toward the great hall. Teetering like a house of cards, the hall's stone walls leaned precariously to one side, daring anyone to come near. Along the walls, rotting tapestries dangled over the huge stone terraces that overlooked an enormous pit of indigo fire which lit the room in shades of blue. At the far end, sat a throne of stone bordered on each side by granite grymalkon cats—their sapphire eyes keenly watching over their domain.

Slowly, the crowd filed in, murmuring as they awaited the arrival of their overlordess. All at once, the flames died to embers as a bitter wind blew through the hall, carrying on it a murder of crows. Converging, they flew to the seat of stone, and morphed into the hideous woman that had been plaguing Paige and Preston for months.

Silent, *She* stared out from beneath her hood and with a wave of her hand, set the smoldering embers ablaze. The crowd quieted as a woman seated on the bottom terrace, moved to the center of the hall. "My liege, Logue has not been heard from for three suns," she said, gazing up at her. "He and Damial were supposed to meet a day past, but for reasons unknown, he did not show. I fear that he may have been run to ground before he could complete his task."

Glancing at her, *She* closed her eyes in thought, and without words, spoke telepathically. *Send a star and two of your order through the tunnels to discover his fate. If they have Logue, we must make haste to retrieve him."*

With a quick nod, the woman gestured toward two men seated near her, and sent them on their way. "My Liege, if we learn that he has indeed been imprisoned, I request that I be allowed to assist in securing his freedom. It would also serve to my benefit as well, since I have unfinished business to attend to—at that mockery they call a school."

Sitting down, *She* stroked her fingers across the head of a stone grymalkon and leaned forward. *"You refer to your brother Auric—yes?"* Solemnly, the woman nodded as she lowered her head. *"So, you desire to avenge his death at the hands of the boy crescent—yes?"* Once more, she nodded in silence. *"All in good time, Maranda—you must remain patient, much as I have had to these last three moons. Be content in knowing that I have plans yet in store for the boy—and an extra share for his meddlesome little sibling. But as time grows late, I am obliged to err on the side of caution, and attend to Logue myself."*

"And what of the girl we have in our possession?" Maranda asked.

She put up a glowing hand and leaned back in her seat, pondering on Elise. *"The girl of the red sun is weak and her mind open to suggestion – I have no doubt that she could be swayed and brought into the fold. Nevertheless, upon reflection, I have a much more useful purpose for her."* Leaping from her high perch, *She* glided down to Maranda's side, shrouded in a blaze of indigo flame. *"A map exists – the girl's jumbled thoughts have revealed this to us. I believe it is the key to what we search for. For six moons, we have scoured his loathsome mountains, yet have found nothing of the bane that swine hid from me. It is a cursed blight that has gnawed at my spine ever since I broke free from his vile prison! For certain, it hides in the shadows – and this map will lead us to where it lies. It is obvious that Logue could not acquire the map, so at this grave impasse, the girl's value is immeasurable. If we use her obvious affection for the boy crescent to our advantage, we can force their hand and lure him in at the same time, bringing us much closer to our quarry."*

Chapter Nineteen

Midnight Ultimatum

Preston stared idly at the chalkboard, desperate to keep his mind on Precept Dryden's lecture, but the harder he tried, the more his mind wandered. Ever since he found out that Elise had been snatched from under his nose, he spent every waking moment thinking about her. But the cruelest reminder of all turned out to be the very class he was sitting in right now—Esoteric-Studies #7. It seemed like only yesterday that he'd peered through the auditorium doors and saw Elise for the very first time.

"Mr. Brandymire?" Precept Dryden asked as the bell rang. "Before you leave, I need to speak to you for a minute." Shrugging, Preston sat down in the front row as the precept leaned against his desk. "Preston, I know you've had it pretty rough of late, and because of that, I've tried to let things slide a bit, but now it appears as if you've lost interest in my class, and your grades are slipping as a result. Under the circumstances, I guess I can't blame you, but what concerns me is that you've been bottling things up inside, and that's never good, is it?"

Giving him a pained expression, Preston fidgeted and took a deep breath. "No, sir, it's not—but nobody's even trying to find Elise. A whole week's gone by, and all they're doing is waiting around."

"Preston, it's easy to see why you feel this way, but to say that no one is trying—well, it's just not true. We're doing everything we can to bring Elise home, even though it might not seem that way to you."

Preston frowned at him and put his hands to his face. "I don't know what to think anymore. I mean, none of this would have happened if it wasn't for me."

Sitting down next to Preston, Precept Dryden shook his head at him. "Maybe you could have prevented this and maybe not, but blaming yourself makes no sense. Look, I'll make a deal with you. If you'll try to concentrate in class, I'll keep you up-to-date on any changes in Elise's situation, how's that sound?"

Instantly, Preston perked up and nodded as the precept handed him a card.

SAMIEL DRYDEN, O.R.F.

PRECEPT, MIDDLE SCHOOL

THE RAYDENCRAFFT CONSERVATORY
FOR THE MENTALLY GIFTED

EXT. 6029

Samiel.Dryden@Raydencrafft.com

"This has my office extension and e-mail address. If you ever need to talk, just give me a call or drop me an e-mail." Mumbling a quick okay, Preston grabbed his bag and followed him to the exit. "Remember—from now on, keep your mind on class. We'll handle the rest together."

As he walked back to his quarters, Preston thought over what Precept Dryden had said. He knew he was right, but still, he couldn't seem to shake the feeling that something worse might happen.

Following the gravel walkway, he reached the top of a grassy rise, stopping as his eyes locked on a group of boys heading his direction. *What do they want? Come to think of it, I don't want to know.* For a split second, he focused on the white shooting star braids on their uniforms, then scowled as he detoured off the path.

Fast approaching, they circled him as the biggest of the five jumped in his face. "Hey, you crescent puke," he snarled, his braces gleaming in the sunlight, "what's your hurry?"

Closing an eye, Preston winced as the boy came within a nose of him. "Oh, come on—I don't need any trouble right now, I'm not in the mood."

"Oh, he's *not* in the *mood.* Well, boo-hoo," he cackled as his pals played along, "you're the one who's causing trouble." Narrowing his icy green gaze, he ran a hand through his jet black hair. "What really gets me is how everyone thinks you're so great, when all you did was lose Elise and nothing else!" Furious, Preston ran at him, only to be thrown to the ground by one the boy's goons. Laughing, the glowering ring leader loomed over Preston and pointed a finger at him. "I just don't get it, she wouldn't even give me the time of day, and then she picks a loser like you—what a joke. And to think she's probably dead because of you!"

Preston stared up at him as he fought to get to his feet, but every time he tried, the bully shoved him back to the ground. "High and mighty crescents, yeah, right," he snarled, shaking his fist. "You and your mealy-mouthed sister are just a couple of charity cases."

With a collective grunt from his buddies, the boy smiled as he pressed his foot hard against Preston's back. "At this school, Shooting Stars sit on the top of the totem pole—you better remember that or you'll be eating dirt again. Oh, and one more thing, I almost didn't get on a Pryttonn team after you and your brat sister messed up the tryouts, so from now on, stay out of my way—or you'll be sorry." As he reared back to kick Preston, he threw a smug look at his pals, then froze. "Oh, crud! Watch out!" he shouted. "Run!" Scrambling, they took off running as a barrage of blazing red fireballs flew past Preston. On the rise, Wil Buller stood there roaring with laughter as the boys ran for their lives.

"That should keep you jerks busy for awhile," Wil yelled. "Besides, you guys could use some exercise." Pulling Preston up from the ground, he flashed him a giant sized grin. "Hey, I see the *little lord* and his gang of delinquents were trying to make friends the only way they know how. What did you do—step on his red carpet?"

"I'm not sure what I did. I was minding my own business and WHAM—he's in my face. Who is he? I've never even seen him before."

Smirking, Wil patted Preston on the back. "*That* was his holiness, Quinten Wickvane—a real blue-blooded jerk of jerks, if you know what I mean. His family's got their name plastered all over this place, and not only that, his father's the dean of the high school."

Preston rolled his eyes as he chased his scattered homework across the grass. "Great, this is perfect. Now I've got a glowing-glob-of-goo, a couple of rotten shifters, *and* a rich kid after me. What's next, someone's rabid dog? Geez, I should sell tickets."

Chuckling at Preston's short list, Wil glanced around the area, and pointed toward their quarters. "Ummm, we'd better go before they figure out those were just vapor spheres I tossed at them. But hey, they really did look like the real thing, didn't they? Oh, and don't worry about running into Quinten any time soon, most of the time he stays at his dad's house in Deatherage—he's way too *good* to sleep with us low-lifes."

"Uh, that's the first good news I've heard in awhile," Preston said, sighing. "I just hope you don't get in trouble for helping me."

Shaking his head, Wil laughed it off. "If the little lord and his goon squad rat on me, they'll have to explain what they were doing out here. And I'm telling you right now, they don't have the brains to think up even a bad story."

As they climbed the steps of the boy's building, thunder rumbled across the campus from far overhead. "Whoa, did you see that? Lightning—over there, above those hills," Preston said as Wil craned his neck to see. "I didn't hear anything about a storm coming, did you?" Wil shrugged and pulled open the doors as Preston stopped and stared at the black clouds on the horizon. *Boy, it's definitely heading this way. I don't know – something just doesn't feel right.*

Pete Jeffries sat on the steps outside campus security, watching streaks of lightning dance across the sky. *One more hour and I'm out of here,* he thought as he stepped inside and locked the doors behind him.

Walking down the hall, he checked each room as he headed for his office, then heard a knock at the door. "Chancellor Manderlane?" he asked, hurrying to the entrance. "You didn't mention you were coming by."

The chancellor smiled and pointed to the rear of the building. "Something's been nagging me about our guest. I need to talk to him again—but alone this time, then perhaps, I'll have some good news once I'm finished." Leaving the chancellor to his task, Pete walked back to his office, and gazed unenthusiastically at the mountain of paperwork on his desk.

KA-RRRANG! All of a sudden, a huge explosion rocked the building, sending chucks of cement and plaster raining down on him as the ceiling gave way. With nowhere to run, he hit the ground only to be buried beneath a shower of debris.

Amid a blast of indigo light, the tangled ruins erupted as Chancellor Manderlane and the dark-shifter emerged from the teetering rubble. Walking out into the open, they stopped as a security team came running up the path. Instantly, the sentries hurled a net of red fire at them, and stood their ground as the spiraling web homed in on its target. Countering their attack, the chancellor froze the net in mid-air, letting it crash to the ground in thousands of ice-blue shards. "You puny pathetic ants, your tricks are useless," he shouted. "Go hide in your holes before I crush you like bugs."

In answer, one of the sentries launched a wave of energy in their direction as the other let loose a machine-gun volley of molten plasma orbs. Batting the fiery globes away, Chancellor Manderlane unleashed a roaring wall of flame at them, and seconds later, it smashed into the guard's energy field, reducing it to nothing. Overpowered, they ran as the blazing wall swallowed them up in a blue inferno.

Without a sound, the chancellor stood over the two unconscious sentries, finally discarding his charade. Staring down at them, *She* raised a glowing hand in the air and smiled. "Now you see, as your end looms near, your efforts were all in vain. It is a pity to die—simply for a matter of one's own pride."

Suddenly, a buzzing sound filled the air as a mass of emerald locusts dove down at her, covering her in a living cocoon of insects. All at once, *She* spun her body around, flinging them off her as the locusts spiraled into a whirlwind, taking on the form of the *real* Chancellor Manderlane. "You! How you managed to cheat your fate defies belief!" Mathias yelled. "I'll be more than happy to throw you back into that hole you climbed out of—the first chance I get!"

Her indigo eyes smoldered as *She* glared at him, then defiantly, *She* turned and waved off her dark-shifter. "Leave, Logue, I'll take care of this fool." Peering at the chancellor, Logue spat at him and leapt into the air, escaping into the night as several sentries and precepts came running toward them. Incensed, *She* hissed at the crowd, raising a fiery fist at Mathias.

"Crescent trash, I grow tired of this game. Suffice it to say, I have only two purposes for being here. One is now complete," *She* screamed, pointing a glowing finger at him. "*You* will complete the other for me. The map—the one your precious crescent siblings conjured up—I desire it. Bring it—*and* the boy—to the western border of the Valley of Darkness by the dawn of the eighth sun or I will kill the girl. Have I made my meaning clear?"

Mathias shook his head and scowled at her. "You're insane. My mind spins to think of the twisted plans you've concocted."

Scornfully, *She* sneered at him, and morphed into an exact duplicate of Elise. "Heed my words. If you ever wish to see the girl again," *She* shouted in Elise's voice, "then I suggest you bring the boy along—or she dies." Dissolving into a murky mist, *She* vanished, leaving them all standing there amid the destruction.

Chapter Twenty

Circle of Three

"Seven days!" Natewick bellowed, pacing the room. "Mathias, that's impossible. There's hardly a way to find the missing map pieces in that small amount of time. And what of Preston Brandymire—ya're not suggesting that we put the boy in harm's way by using him as a pawn in this wicked business, are ya?"

"Natewick, I realize this is an obvious trap, but our first priority must be to locate the rest of the map. Anything we might do after that is moot at this point."

"Well, far be it for me to be worrying about the boy's wellbeing," the little man said sarcastically. "So, ya're right, we should just toss him to the lions since this map is so awfully important to be stressing about anything else."

Mathias stopped in mid-step and glared at him. "*That* was

uncalled for," he snapped as Natewick stood his ground. "Face it—there isn't a painless way out of this."

Retrieving Paige and Preston's map pieces, Mathias projected an image of them onto a monitor. "For the past few weeks, I've been analyzing these, and I believe I've found something extraordinary to say the least," he said, pointing to a section of the map. "There, do you see that?"

Natewick's eyes narrowed as he wrinkled his nose at the screen. "What is it? It looks like gibberish to me."

"It's far from that. In fact, I believe it's some sort of numbered code—a three hundred year old code to be exact—hidden in the parchment." At a complete loss for words, the little man gave him a blank stare. "Natewick, don't you see? The map's a diversion—a fake, designed to throw off everyone except the person it was intended for. Each set of numbers could refer to a global position or something as simple as text in a book. The missing pieces must make reference to them."

Natewick gazed at the numeric jumble on the screen, fidgeting in place as his frustration grew. "This is all well and good, but none of it explains to me where the other pieces are or what this gibberish means."

"You're right, but the map isn't the only thing *She's* after," Mathias said, drumming his fingers on the table. "*She* wants something from these children as well. That said, I feel our next step is to talk to them as soon as possible."

The morning sun rose up over the hills, inching its way into the window of chamber 3-17. Pulling their blankets over their heads, the three girls groaned in perfect chorus.

It's only five-thirty. Is it just me or is the sun coming up way too early? Aubree thought as she peered out the window. With a sigh, she tried to focus on the blanket-covered lumps in the other beds. Burying her face back in her pillow, she peeked out at them. "Hey, what do you think happened last night? It sounded like the Fourth of July." In response, both lumps grumbled and shifted in place, but stayed under cover. Aubree sandwiched her face in her hands and frowned at the two grumpy girls. "Well, you might not be curious, but I am." Dragging herself into the bathroom, she poked her head out. "You know, you guys aren't going to be able to get back to sleep. Besides, the alarm's going to go off soon."

Terrin pulled the covers off and scowled at her. "Aubree—if you keep talking, we definitely won't. And as for last night, I couldn't see any more than you could, so why are you asking me?"

Ignoring her, Aubree finished her morning ritual, making an abrupt stop at their chamber door. "Hey, who's this for?" she asked, picking up an envelope from the floor. "Paige, someone left you a note."

Paige shot up and stared at her. "This better not be a joke, because I'm—" she griped, squinting at the envelope. "Hey, you're not joking." Mystified, she opened it carefully and gazed at the contents.

From the desk of

NATEWICK BEADLE

Dear Paige:

Chancellor Manderlane and I have made arrangements for you and Preston to be excused from classes today. Please meet us at Manderlane Hall after breakfast at 9 a.m.

Best,

Natewick

NATEWICK

"What—huh—how? Terrin, you'll never believe this," Aubree sputtered. "Paige gets the day off." Rapidly, her face went pale as an awful thought came to her. "Wait a second—you aren't in *trouble,* are you? Gee, I hope that's not why you're going—uh, what did you do?"

Paige's eyes widened as she threw her hands up in the air and scowled. "Aubree, I didn't do anything. At least I don't think so, but maybe Preston did. Oh, tell me I didn't say that, he didn't do anything either."

In a huff, Terrin launched out of bed and glared at them. "I'm sorry, I really don't care if you robbed a bank. All I want to do is get a little more sleep without someone blabbing in my ear."

Avoiding Terrin's wrath, Aubree and Paige slipped back into bed, and stared up at the ceiling as Paige brooded over the real purpose of Natewick's note. And as everyone dozed off, the shrill sound of the six-thirty alarm ricocheted off the walls. Slapping the snooze button, Terrin slipped out of bed first, grumbling as she made her way to the bathroom.

"I told you it was going to go off," Aubree said as Terrin slammed the door in reply. Shrugging, Aubree slid out of bed, then grabbed her backpack as she gave Paige a glum look. "I'll miss you in class today. Remember, I want to hear all about it later, okay?"

The ten minute walk after breakfast seemed to go on forever. Gazing up at the doors of Manderlane Hall, Preston closed an eye and considered yet another try at them, opting for the intercom instead. "Yes—may I help you?" a woman's voice shot from the speaker.

With an awkward stumble, Preston sputtered into the intercom. "Uh...ummm, I'm Preston Brandymire. Me and my sister are here to see Chancellor Manderlane and Head Counsel Beadle."

After a short pause, the doors opened. "The head counsel will meet you on the fourth floor," the woman added as the speaker crackled. "Just use the lift at the far end of the hall."

At the elevator, Paige pressed the fourth floor button and took a deep breath. "Preston, my stomach feels awful. I hate this—I hate not knowing what's going on."

"Hey, come on, we can't be sure what this is about—it probably isn't anything," he said in a gallant attempt to reassure her. "Besides, remember what Mom told us? As long as we stick together we'll be all right."

At last, the elevator slowed to a stop, and as they stepped out, Natewick greeted them. "Missy, I'm pleased to see ya again—and Preston, how have ya been doing?"

"Okay, I guess. Ummm, Mr. Beadle, what's going on?"

Closing an eye, the little man smiled at him. "Well, I'll have to leave that for the chancellor to explain, it's a tad bit complicated, ya see."

"It's about last night, isn't it? At breakfast, everyone was talking about the chemistry department blowing up."

"The *Chemistry* department?" Natewick chuckled. "Now, I've heard many a tall tale in my life, but this one takes the prize for the most preposterous."

Preston ran his hand through his hair and grinned. "Yeah, I guess that sounds pretty stupid, doesn't it? But there's the alien assault theory—did you want to hear that one?" Natewick winked impishly at Paige and patted Preston on the shoulder, then led them to the chancellor's office.

As they entered, Chancellor Manderlane got up from his chair. "Paige, it's always a pleasure." She gave him a bright smile and managed a soft thank you in return. Shifting his gaze to Preston, Mathias stared keenly at him. "And you, young man, I have to apologize for taking this long to meet you. Sadly, things never seem to settle down enough around here for me to get any free time." Sitting down, he threw Natewick a quick glance and got straight to the point. "So, I'm sure you're curious as to why we asked you to come," he said, leaning forward in his chair. "I regret that there's no easy way to say this, but the circumstances surrounding your friend Elise Temberly have changed considerably."

Pulling no punches, he poured out the details of the previous night, ending with the woman's mind-boggling ultimatum. "—so the situation has reached a critical turning point and we have to act soon."

Paige and Preston grew ghostly pale as they sat there in utter silence. Shaking his head, Preston's face went from white to red in an instant. "Sir, this glob-lady's off her rocker. *She* doesn't care about Elise—*She'll* just get her rotten hands on the map and kill her."

Tapping a pen against his desk, Mathias gazed thoughtfully at Preston. "The other day, Precept Dryden and I met for dinner, during which he touched on the fact that you had a rather fiery way of putting things. At the time, I felt that he must have been exaggerating, but now I find it's true."

Preston frowned and dropped his head. "I'm sorry, sir. I should have kept my big mouth shut."

"Nonsense, I find your brand of honesty quite refreshing, but enough of that—let's address the points you brought up. First of all, this woman can't be trusted, and there's a tremendous danger in dealing with her. However, we need to focus on a more pressing problem, specifically the map."

Paige glanced nervously at Preston and Natewick, then wrinkled her nose at Mathias. "But, sir—uh, I don't understand—how can we help? We didn't even know what we were doing when we found the pieces in the first place."

"That's true, but I believe I've found a solution to this," he said, laying his hand on the desk. "Paige, do you remember when we met and shook hands?" Smiling, she nodded as Preston made a face at her. "What happened puzzled me at first, but then I realized that there must be a connection between us because we're both crescents. I'm almost certain it's in this link that we can find the remaining pieces."

Raising his brow, Natewick gazed at the siblings and pointed a quivering finger at Mathias. "Now wait a single minute, ya're not proposing a bonding of your minds, are ya? It's never been done before and could be dangerous to say the least."

Awkwardly, Preston and Paige stared at each other until Preston finally spoke up. "Mr. Beadle, that doesn't matter to me. If it'll help Elise, I'll do it," he said, turning to Paige for support. "We've got to do something—anything."

"Natewick, I really think Preston's right," Paige said uneasily, "but still, it scares me that I have to have another bad dream just so we can get the rest of the pieces."

Giving her a look of encouragement, Mathias moved to the front of his desk and leaned against it. "Paige, what I'm proposing really can't be described as a normal dream—it's more like being in a trance. Furthermore, Natewick would monitor our progress. So, if things get out of hand, he can choose to end the process safely. As for my part, I'll be there to oversee things." With a wave of his hand, he opened a concealed doorway. "Okay, if you'll follow me, we'll get started."

As Preston followed them through the hidden compartment, he gawked at the menagerie of odd contraptions. Stopping by a strange brass apparatus, he studied the jumble of tubes and wires, frowning as he read the gold nameplate.

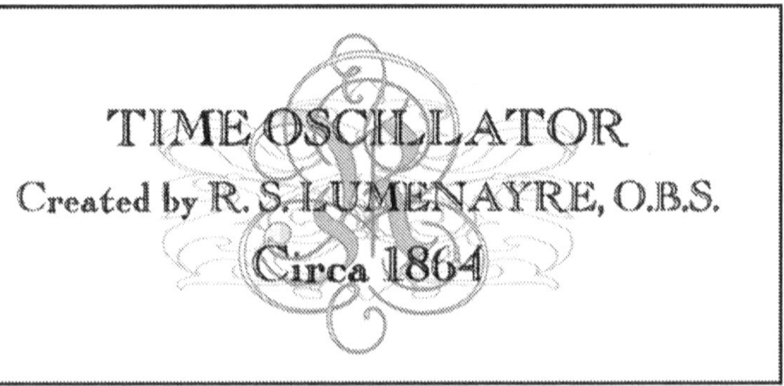

TIME OSCILLATOR
Created by R. S. LUMENAYRE, O.B.S.
Circa 1864

Time Oscillator? Lumenayre? Geez, I can't stand it. Who doesn't have their name plastered all over this place?

Weaving through the conference area, they entered an adjoining drawing room. A cauldron of emerald fire rested in the center of the room atop a large stone pedestal, its light flickering off the walls. *Whoa – a cauldron? Boil – boil – toil and trouble,* Preston mused. *And spooky green fire? Weird.*

Leading them to a small, round table, Mathias pulled out a chair for Paige, then as they all sat down, the flames turned to cinders. "Okay, the first thing we need to do is complete a circle," he instructed. "Whatever you do, don't let go, no matter what."

As Mathias offered his hands to Paige and Preston, an antique clock ticked quietly in the background, its pendulum keeping perfect time with Preston's heartbeat. All the while, Natewick gripped the armrests of his chair as he watched from a few feet away. "All right, here we go," Mathias said as they closed the circle. "Remember, hold on tight."

TICK—TICK—TICK—TICK—the tinny sound of the clock thundered through Preston's brain. Sweat began to trickle down his face as each clang of the clock grew louder. *I can't do this, that sound!* All at once, everything lit up in a burst of brilliant light as hundreds of emerald orbs swirled around the room, surrounding the circle of three in a huge sparkling sphere. Suddenly, a flurry of indigo globes surfaced from within the energy field, orbiting it like electrons around an atom—then came a thunderous boom, followed by dead silence.

Chapter Twenty-One

Valley of the Emerald Sky

"Paige! Chancellor Manderlane!" Preston shouted. "Anybody!" Standing at the edge of a cliff, he shaded his eyes and stared out over the valley. High above, the sun hid behind a curtain of green haze as a sky full of clouds flew swiftly across the horizon. "What is this place? And where'd everybody go?"

Carefully, he followed the rocky path down until he came to a dead-end. Peering out over the ridge of a deep ravine, he shook his head and scowled. "Great, now what am I going to do?" he said, gazing up the mountainside. "It's too far to the top, I'll never make it. Uh, I guess I could always *fly* up there. Yeah, that'll be easy—a piece of cake." *Sure, just keep saying that and maybe you'll believe it,* he thought, then climbed back to where he started. "Chancellor Manderlane! Paige! Where are you?"

In answer, a soft voice rolled over the cliff-side. "You must learn to rely on yourself—your life and the lives of those you care for depend upon it." At Preston's feet, a shimmering emerald fog crawled along the cliff and spiraled upwards in front of him, slowly taking on the likeness of Damon Raydencrafft. "Great adversity lies before you. Take heed, for *She* has yet to realize that you are but one part of the key *She* seeks. Blinded by her undying hate, *She* cannot see this."

With a whirling motion, Damon reached out his hand as hundreds of misty tendrils sprouted from it, transforming into a sparkling green leather-bound journal. "This link of the chain must now be set in place." Handing Preston the book, he pointed to the valley below. "There, lies the site of the conservatory, but in this time construct, only the assembly hall and the library are near completion." Damon's vaporous apparition gazed up at the sky as if he'd sensed something on the wind, and then slowly began to dissolve away. "Your companions approach. Remember, time closes in on you—search below for the answers you seek—it is but the first step in the perilous journey that lies ahead." The voice faded, leaving a mere whisper on the wind as Preston stared at the journal.

"Preston?" Paige called out from above. "Where are you?"

Covering his eyes, he squinted to see through the garish light of the veiled sun. "Paige, I'm down here," he shouted, waving his arms wildly. "Is Chancellor Manderlane with you?"

Mathias peered down at him and smiled. "Preston, I'm here," he yelled, giving Paige a look of reassurance. "Sorry it took so long for us to find you, I'm afraid we encountered a few obstacles along the way. Hold on, we'll come down to you."

Effortlessly, he shifted into a giant red griffon, and lowered a wing for Paige. Getting on his back, she grabbed a handful of feathers, and quickly, they floated down to Preston's ledge, and lifted him skyward. "Preston, hang on," he crowed as they soared high above the valley. "Don't worry, we'll be on solid ground soon."

As they flew downward, the countryside rushed past them in a blur of green and brown. Gliding inches above the ground, Mathias dropped Preston in the high grass, then set down a few feet away from him. Preston dusted himself off, closing an eye as he smirked at the chancellor's feathery guise. "Boy, I really thought I was stuck up there, and WOOSH—you turn into *Big Bird* just like that," he said as Mathias returned to human form. "Hey, I'm not complaining, but I still can't figure out how these things work at all."

Mathias grinned as he glanced up at the horizon. "Preston, these things take time. But if you consider what we've achieved just by being here, it's truly extraordinary."

"Yeah, but...uh, there's something I've got to tell you," he said, handing the journal to him. "I got another special delivery."

Taking the book, Mathias leafed through it, then rubbed the back of his neck. "Unbelievable, this is one of Damon's personal journals. But, the bulk of them disappeared long ago—how did you find it?"

"Well, ummm, I didn't actually *find* it," Preston explained, giving Mathias an uneasy look, "he gave it to me, sort of."

At a loss for words, Mathias studied the pages, then stopped on a dime as he gazed up at Demora Hall. "Strange, Damon's written here that the remaining pieces are hidden within the hall and the library, yet these specific locations no longer exist in the present. My best guess is that the pieces can only be found within this ripple in time. Okay then, let's head to the library, but stay together and don't wander off."

Traveling along the river's edge, Mathias pointed out the

landmarks he recognized as Paige and Preston gawked at one strange sight after another. As they reached the crest of a sloping grassy hill, the library finally came into view. From where Preston stood, the building didn't appear to be any different, but outside there was no memorial or garden in the front square, only weeds and dirt. "Ummm, what did they do—fire the gardener?" he quipped. "Miss Picklesimer would have a fit if she saw this. Heck, even by my standards it's a dump."

Giggling, Paige gave the chancellor a coy smile. "He's telling the truth. You should see his room back at our house. My mom's still trying to get the pizza stains out of the carpet."

Preston made a face at her as Mathias laughed and stared up at the entrance. "One of the pieces is hidden in the rooftop atrium. It might be a bit tricky to reach, so you two should wait by the entrance." Walking up the steps, they entered the library, pausing inside the doorway. "All right, I'll be back in a few minutes," he said, pointing down at their feet. "Stay right here."

As Mathias walked away, Preston eyed the front desk and smirked. "I wonder if Miss Picklesimer's hiding behind there," he said with a chuckle. "Hey, you want to look around a little?"

Paige's eyes widened. "Preston, he told us to stay here."

Avoiding her stare, he took a few steps past the desk, and poked his head down a dark aisle. "Geez, the whole place is empty—now, this is way too creepy." *Whoa! Huh? Something moved back there.* Stopping dead in his tracks, he tensed up as he peered into the shadows. "Chancellor Manderlane?" No answer. "Who's there?" Not a sound. Slowly, he backed away and bolted towards the entrance. Turning the corner, he skidded to a stop as Mathias stepped in front of him.

"Didn't I tell you to stay where you were?"

"Yeah—you did," Preston sputtered, glancing nervously in the direction of where he heard the sounds, "but there's someone back there."

Following Preston, Mathias checked each of the empty aisles, then frowned. "Uh, there's no one here. Preston, I realize you're curious, but next time, do us all a favor and stay put, okay?"

As they reached the entrance, Paige shook her head at Preston. "I told you not to go back there, but you wouldn't listen to me."

He glared at her as Mathias stepped between them. In his hand, he held another piece of the map. "I found this hidden in the brickwork," he explained, slipping it into his bag. "We'd better go—our quest ends at Demora Hall."

Staring up at Demora Hall's stained glass dome, Preston and Paige walked across the bare lobby, stopping in front of the main hall's entrance. Above the large entryway, Demora Raydencrafft, draped in satin and lace, gazed down at them from her portrait.

"Who's she?" Paige asked as Preston wrinkled his nose at the painting.

"Her name was Demora," Mathias answered as he opened the doors to the assembly hall, "she was Damon's half-sister."

"Demora? Preston—uh, doesn't she look a lot like Mom?" she whispered. "And her eyes, they're just like yours."

Shrugging it off, Preston walked to the doorway and peered in. "So—what do we do now?"

"The way into the basement is at the far end," Mathias said, pointing as he ignited his hands, "follow me and stay together." Carefully, they inched their way to the rear of the hall, stopping as the floor creaked beneath their feet. "Wait—do you hear that?" Stomping against the floorboards, he knelt down and waved his hand across the floor. "Right here—there's a hidden panel."

Throwing it open, he led them down the stairs, then guided them through a maze of cobwebs and crates. At the back of the basement, Mathias knelt down and counted the brickwork from top to bottom. Wiping off the surface, he counted across from his left, and pressed hard against the eighth brick. All of a sudden, a section of the wall fell away, revealing a secret compartment. "What's that?" Preston asked as they all stared at a small stone box. "Hey, it looks like King Tut's tomb, only way smaller." The cover had an engraved pair of crescent moons, each surrounded by a circle linked to one another by an intertwining carved rope.

"It's another one of Damon's fail-safes," Mathias said. "These symbols indicate the presence of a dual interlocking shield." Placing his hand above the sarcophagus, he jerked it back just as a field of shimmering energy enveloped the box. "According to Damon's journal, it can only be unlocked by two people at the same time, but not just any two people. Specifically, they have to be crescent siblings—a brother and sister."

"What? You want *us*—to touch *that?*" Paige exclaimed. "Oh, I don't think so."

Preston scowled at her. "Paige, it's the only way we can help Elise. You know I can't do it without you."

In tears, she turned to Mathias, kneading her hands as she gazed at him. "Okay, what do we have to do?"

Mathias put his hands above the vault and looked at them. "Preston needs to put his left hand here and you'll place yours there," he explained, pointing at the two circles, "that should release the lock."

Sliding in front of the lockbox, they glanced nervously at each other. "Paige—when I count to three, we'll put our hands down, okay?" Preston asked. Wincing, she nodded. "Okay, one—two—THREE." In unison, they closed their eyes and pressed their hands to the circles.

Nothing's happening – nothing's changed. Cracking open an eye, Preston found an emerald pool of molten magma welling up over their hands as it filled the carved recesses of the stone. Seconds later, the glowing lava vanished, and after a series of clicks and clanks, the vault's cover slid open.

Reaching inside, Mathias brought out yet another journal. Page after page, he searched through it, finally pulling out the last piece of the map. Stowing their prize in his bag for safe keeping, he led them back to the stairs, then stopped and raised a finger to his lips. "Wait," he whispered, holding them back with his arm, "something's not right—don't move." Cautiously, he climbed the stairs and peered into the dark assembly hall. Moving his blazing hand in a tight circular motion, he spun the spiraling flames into a fiery spear and hurled it at the ceiling, illuminating the entire room.

"Get to the back of the basement," he shouted down at them. Gripping the floorboards, his arms bulged as he began to shift. "Now!"

Horrified, Preston and Paige watched as Mathias was yanked through the opening. Backpedaling, they spun around and ran to the back wall. Above them, the frenzied battle raged on as Preston looked up at the highest step. "Paige—up there—the chancellor's bag. We've got to get it before they do."

"Preston—no! What if they see you?"

Holding a hand up, he stared at the bag with grim resolve. "You know what's going to happen if *She* gets her hands on it, don't you? Elise is as good as dead." Slowly, he crept up the steps and reached for the bag, when unexpectedly, it became deathly quiet. Grabbing the bag, Preston secured it over his shoulder, and jumped back down to Paige.

Overhead, the wood rafters creaked under the weight of footsteps. Suddenly, the woman of their nightmares glared down at them, her flaming indigo eyes piercing the black void. "Yes—the crescent younglings—I thought I felt your presence. Hiding below will serve no purpose, there is no way out—you are trapped. And since your *mentor* is the only one who can release you from this pathetic mock world, you haven't any choice but to come up." Without a word, Preston pulled Paige towards the back of the basement, then wheeled around, and focused on the opening. "Crescent whelps! I warn you—do not test my patience!"

"Hey, you'll have to come down here and get us," Preston yelled as his eyes began to smolder, "because we're staying right where we are!"

With a blood curdling shriek, *She* ripped through the floorboards and flew down the stairs in a fiery rage as Preston stood in front of Paige and held his ground. All at once, the aura around him exploded, showering the walls from ceiling to floor in molten gel. Turning to liquid, the brickwork dissolved away in a muddy waterfall, bringing the entire hall down around them.

"You wretched little fools," *She* screeched, "you think this is the end? It is only the beginning!" Spinning around like a top, *She* dematerialized into a glowing cloud of dust at the exact moment a huge wooden beam smashed through the ceiling above her.

Desperately, Preston tried to throw a shield around them as a torrent of debris came pouring down from above. Grabbing Preston, Paige let out a scream and cringed as everything turned a brilliant white, and then—went dark.

"Wha…what happened? Are ya all right?" Natewick exclaimed, staring wide-eyed at them. "Ya were all thrashing about so much, that I thought ya were going to hurt yourselves, so I pulled ya back."

Speechless, they gazed at each other as Mathias groaned. "The bag—I left it behind."

Preston shook his head. "Sir, I've got it. I grabbed it off the stairs," he said, setting the bag in the middle of the table. "Boy, I don't know how you guys feel, but what's in this bag better be all we need, because as far as field trips go, this is the last one I ever want to take."

Chapter Twenty-Two

The Dawn of the Eighth Sun

Thousands of tiny pin pricks of light sparkled in the night sky as Preston lay there letting his thoughts drift from star to star. After stopping to rest their horses on the way to the markers of the Valley of Darkness, he had been waiting impatiently for a word from Mathias. Any word—so that they could break camp and start the last leg of the journey.

"Chancellor Manderlane?" Sitting up, Preston stared awkwardly at Mathias. "You know who this woman is that's chasing us, don't you?"

The campfire flickered in Mathias' eyes as he put his back against a broken tree trunk and gave Preston a look of resignation. "Preston, did you know that Damon was a crescent?" he asked as Preston shook his head. "Well, the same was true of his half-sister.

Although they had that in common, they couldn't have been anymore different, even if they'd tried. Because of these differences, Demora's resentment towards him grew to hatred. So, in the end, it was his own sister who betrayed him."

Breathing in the cool air, Mathias warmed his hands over the fire, and put them to his face. "Soon after, Demora renounced the name of Raydencrafft, condemning the crescent order as a charade. And from there, *She* embarked on a murderous spree that went on for years, each time deriving greater pleasure from doing the unspeakable. If not for Damon, the plague of pain and death Demora wrought upon the Emerald Mountains would have gone unchecked for years to come. We can only be thankful, that he and the remaining members of his fellowship succeeded in stopping her. But now, through a turn of wicked luck, *She*'s somehow managed to escape from the prison of her brother's making, only to seek revenge against those responsible for her imprisonment—namely, the order of the crescent."

Getting to his feet, Mathias gathered their camping gear and packed it away as Preston gaped at him. "Demora has always been a black cloud looming over these mountains. *She* is instinct alone, thoroughly incapable of any remorse. On the lowest rung, Demora's a cruel and sadistic animal. If we hadn't brought you and your sister to the conservatory, I'm sure *She* would have done serious harm to you both, sooner than later."

As Mathias helped him up onto his horse, Preston frowned and pulled down the brim of his cap. "But—how can we even trust her? What if *She* tries to fool us again? I mean, how would we even know?"

Glancing at Preston out of the corner of his eye, Mathias gripped his horse's reins and stared down the trail. "Preston, as you gain more experience, your abilities will improve, so much so, that you can read a person's emotions. Somehow, Demora and her followers are resistant to this, but in Elise's case, I'm sure I'll know if they've made a switch."

Great, all he has to do is read a few minds, Preston thought as they moved up the path, *and then he'll know they've made a switch—yeah, right. And what about these markers he keeps taking about?* As far as he could figure, they had to be right smack dab in the middle of some weird no-man's land—a place where everything fell off the side of the earth. Squirming in his saddle, Preston rocked his head from side to side as he pondered over his meager choices. "Ummm, how much farther do we have to go?"

"We're about an hour out," Mathias said. "If everything goes as planned, we should reach the border well before sunrise. That should give us enough time to ready ourselves."

"Preston—down there," Mathias said, pointing to the clearing below. "The warning markers, we're here." In the moonlight, a vast field of high grass lay before them, bordered by a dense wall of trees. Hundreds of flaming red lamps lined the border, sending an ominous message that something evil lurked beyond them.

From where he sat, Preston watched as Chancellor Manderlane raised his hand to the night sky. From his fingertips, fiery tendrils flowed outward as he spun them like a lasso. Launching the blazing whips into the air, Mathias glanced up at the hovering strands of light, then out over the edge. "That should provide us plenty of light for now. Remember, once we're down in the grass, stay as close to these cliffs as possible."

Cautiously, Mathias guided Preston down a series of

switchbacks, splitting his attention between the path and the tree-line. Reaching the clearing, they looked out over the grasslands, focusing on the glowing markers. "We're running short on time," Mathias said as they jumped down from their horses, "we'd better get started."

As he gripped Preston's hands and closed his eyes, a cloud of sparkling mist swept around them, and then seamlessly, they switched places with one another. Staring at his carbon copy, Preston put a hand to his new face and scowled. "Geez, I don't know if I can do this."

"Preston, relax—*She's* after me, because I'm you, remember? Try to say as little as possible and you'll be fine," he instructed. "Just don't forget the part you're playing, we can't afford to give ourselves away." Moving around in his new skin, Mathias walked towards the markers, then turned to Preston. "Demora's probably going to bring along an entourage. So, keep sharp, because things might get a bit tricky."

On the horizon, a golden sliver of light peeked out over the trees, heralding the sun's arrival. Quickly, Mathias threw a blazing vapor sphere over Preston's hands, and positioned himself behind him. "They're coming—stay in front of me." From above, a group of giant winged lizards fast approached, swooping down to show them a brief glimpse of their cargo.

"Elise!" Preston yelled as Mathias grabbed his arm. Holding her tightly in their grasp, the shifters set down under the cover of the forest, dragging her behind them as they emerged from the thicket. Among the five dark-shifters, one stood out from the rest. "It's that woman from the tunnels!" Preston said, clenching his fists.

Glaring at Mathias' boyish disguise, she stood silent as an impenetrable fog crept from the forest, carrying on it scores of spider-like bats. A lab experiment gone wrong, the hideous creatures thrashed about as they gathered into a black mass of wings and legs, then melded effortlessly into *She.* Motionless, Demora's eyes darted from Mathias to Preston's glowing hands. "Am I to assume from your unfriendly posture that you—*distrust* me? Oh, how it distresses me that you would feel that way after we were off to such a grand beginning," *She* said contemptuously. "Well, such are the times in which we live. Be that as it may, it is a shame that these unfortunate misunderstandings happen from time to time, don't you agree?"

"Whatever! Let's get this over with," Preston shouted as he pulled the map from Mathias' bag and held it in the air. "Here's your map—now give us Elise."

Gesturing to one of her underlings, *She* shot a fiery look at Preston as they pushed Elise to the forefront. "Here is the girl. Have the boy bring the map and I will free her."

"What? You must think I'm stupid! He's staying right where he is—I'll bring it!"

"No! The boy brings it," *She* said, wrapping her gruesome fingers around Elise's neck, "or I will kill her in a manner most unpleasant."

Hearing her threat, Mathias stepped out into the open and stared her down. "Fine—leave her alone," he said, then whispered to Preston. "I'll be okay, just get Elise away from here."

Reluctantly, Preston handed him the map and turned to face her. "When he starts walking, you let her go."

With a wave of her hand, *She* cut Elise's ties, but kept a firm grip around her neck. "Send him—I grow tired of waiting." As Demora and Preston eyed one another from opposite sides, Mathias and Elise began walking towards each other across the meadow. Step by step, they closed in on each other until they were within earshot of one another.

"Preston," Elise whimpered, "I want to go home."

"Elise, listen—keep moving. You'll be fine, I promise you," Mathias said, watching Demora and her henchmen like a hawk. Suddenly, the five dark-shifters broke ranks and took flight, heading directly for them. "Elise—run! Now!" Breathlessly, Mathias bolted across the grasslands on a collision course with Demora, glancing back to see Preston lift Elise off the ground and veer away.

Instantly, Demora's dark-shifters scattered, then spun around and reversed course, but not before Mathias catapulted himself onto her. Staggering backwards, *She* fought to free herself as he threw a straight jacket of emerald plasma around her and tightened his grip. "Demora, you should have crawled back into your hole when you had the chance!" As *She* thrashed about, hundreds of orbs leeched themselves to the energy field, burrowing through to continue their attack from inside.

Following the melee from up high, Maranda, the leader of the dark-shifters, waved off the others and plunged to the ground. CRASH! BOOM! She struck Mathias and Demora, sending them tumbling across the grasslands. Swinging around, she focused her eyes on the clearing—in its center laid the map. Swiftly, she snatched up the patchwork parchment, then set down next to her overlordess as the other shifters disappeared over the forest.

"My liege," Maranda whispered, "I have what you seek." Taking her quarry in hand, Demora glared at Mathias, pointing a defiant finger at him. "Boy, you are truly a needle in my side. Take the girl—she is worthless to me. But, I will leave you with one question to ponder on. Why are you different than your kin? Your pathetic mentor won't dare tell you, but I will—when the time is right."

Suddenly, *She* and Maranda sprouted grotesque wings and lifted off, then hovered above him. "At last, I will be rid of my vile bane—and once I have destroyed it, your pathetic house will be next!" *She* screamed. "Boy, think well of what I've told you—for now, I take my leave." With a cackling shriek, *She* turned and followed Maranda toward the sun, vanishing into the horizon.

Struggling to his feet, Mathias walked gingerly to his mare, leaning up against her as Preston and Elise made their way down to him. "Chancellor Manderlane, are you all right?" Preston asked as he guided his horse across the clearing. "Everything happened so fast, I wasn't sure what to do."

Elise's face went white as she glanced at Mathias. "What? I don't understand. Preston, why did *he* call you that? Oh, please, this can't be a dream. I don't know what I'll do if it is."

Mathias stared quizzically at Elise as Preston jumped down and helped her off the saddle. "Elise, I realize things appear quite upside down at present—it seems I've lost track of some important details," he said using Preston's best grin. "Perhaps, it would be better if I showed you, rather than try to explain it."

Taking each other's hands, he and Preston stood motionless as a fiery explosion of light engulfed them. As they transformed back to their former selves, Elise broke into tears, trembling from head to toe. "Preston? Please tell me it's really you."

"Elise, it's me—really," he whispered, wiping her tears away, "and I'm still crazy about you. Don't ever let anyone tell you otherwise." He took her hand and together they walked his colt over to the base of the cliffs where the chancellor stood gazing at the markers.

"Chancellor Manderlane?" Preston asked. "Is everything

okay?"

Mathias ran his fingers through the high grass and smiled. "Don't worry, everything's fine. These grasslands are full of ghosts and childhood memories for me. To be honest, I'd like to come here one day and see this field for what it is and not for what it was, but that might be asking for quite a lot."

"Ghosts?" Preston said, wrinkling his nose at the dark forest thicket. "Yeah, this place is a creepfest for sure, all it needs is a haunted house parked in the middle of it."

Nodding in agreement, Elise eyed them both anxiously. "I'm just happy to be away from that awful place and those horrible people," she said with a frown. "Oh, can't we go? All I want to do is see my family."

Gently squeezing her hand, Mathias gave them a boost up and then swung himself up onto his mare. "All right, let's get you back to the conservatory, so you can do just that."

Chapter Twenty-Three

The Invisible Boy

Since their return from the markers, things had more or less settled back into a comfortable routine. With each day that passed, the daily trials of making it to class on time and passing the occasional pop quiz became the only things any of them cared to think about.

Trying to act as if everything was normal hadn't been that easy for Preston, seeing that several outrageous stories were making the rounds all over school. But truth or not, it had become painfully clear that everyone either thought of him as some sort of conquering hero or a complete loser who happened to be along for the ride.

During lunch, Preston sat outside with Aaron as Jim and Wil brought their trays to their table. Gazing up at the ocean of blue sky,

Aaron took in a deep breath, and smiled from ear to ear. "No more rain, nada. It's about time, all this rotten weather was getting on my nerves. I just hope it stays this way so I can get through practice."

Jim rolled his eyes and gave Aaron a look of disapproval. "Practice? You know, there's more to life than Pryttonn. I can think of plenty of things to do that don't involve taking a shower afterwards, and you guys won't do any of them." Using his hand as a calculator, he counted off the possibilities. "Video games—remember those? How about movies? We've got a theater, but do we ever use it? And what about tunes? Nothing. But mention some stupid sport and you all start drooling."

Aaron and Wil shrugged as Preston threw his hands up and pleaded the fifth. "That's all you guys have to say?" Jim exclaimed, going red. "Then fine. Just don't come running when you want to play my games again. JR's game store is closed until further notice."

"What's closed?" Paige asked as she and Elise sat down at their table. Making a face, Preston tried to get her off the subject as Aubree and Terrin squeezed in next to them. "What? Oh, wait, you're having one of your moments, aren't you? Then, don't mind us, we'll watch from over here in the stands."

"Stands? See, I told you," Jim shouted as he stared at Paige in bewilderment. "You've all got sports on the brain."

In a fluster, Aaron quickly changed the subject. "So Paige, are you going to tell Preston what you did in Malineus' lab class today?" he asked as her eyes bugged out at him. "What? Come on, tell him. It was great."

Folding her arms, Paige glared at him and looked the other way. "Okay, if you're not going to spit it out, then I will," he said, grinning at Preston. "You know how Precept Malineus likes dissecting things in biology class? Well, today we were supposed to cut open a bunch of rats."

Gasping in chorus, Aubree and Terrin dropped their forks. "Hey, we're trying to eat! That's just plain gross," Aubree grumbled as Terrin and Elise seconded the motion.

"Whatever," Aaron said as Paige turned ten shades of red. "So, we're that close to slicing and dicing our furry little friends when Precept Malineus starts drawing all the gooey little things we're going to find after we did the deed—"

Aubree slammed her fork down and pushed her plate away. "Aaron, are you trying to be annoying, because it's really working."

On a roll, Aaron blew her off as he laughed hysterically. "Now, here's where it *really* gets weird," he cackled. "The minute Precept Malineus has her back turned, Paige sneaks to the back and busts the rats out of their cages. You should have seen it; there were rats everywhere—all over the floor, on the desks, and even in Dori Van Peterslee's hair."

Their mouths fell open as they all stared at Paige, now beet red and fuming at Aaron. "And you want to know what the funniest part was?" he asked. "While all this was going on, Paige was hopping up and down like she'd just won one for rats across America. Gee, it sure didn't seem like Precept Malineus saw it that way, huh, Paige?"

Paige shook her head in despair. "No—she didn't see it my way at all. It's not fair. What they were doing to those rats was wrong, but I should've made up a better plan than that."

Giving her a sympathetic smile, Elise scowled at Aaron. "They shouldn't ask us to cut up little animals. It's not very nice at all—and it's not so nice for the rats, either."

Unable to hold back, Aaron burst out in laughter, slapping his hand down on the table. "Not nice for the rats? You're kidding, right?" he asked, making a face. "You wouldn't be saying that if one of them wound up in bed with you some night. Geez, they're all over the place, don't you know that?"

More squirming broke out as Aaron pointed a finger at Paige, throwing her a devilish grin. "Come on, tell them the punch line, they'll love it."

With a sigh, she looked forlornly at Preston, dropping her shoulders in defeat. "Fine! I got detention! There—are you happy?"

"Not even close," he said, roaring with laughter. "Aren't you forgetting the best part?" Gritting her teeth, Paige refused to utter even a single word as he fit in the final piece of the puzzle. "She has to clean the rat cages after school for a whole week!"

Paige lowered her head and tried to hide her growing shame as Preston chuckled. "Preston?" she shouted. "You're supposed to be on my side."

"I'm sorry, but a rat jailbreak is a real work of genius," he said, trying to keep from laughing. "Hey, but you know what? Your little rodent uprising is going to single-handedly knock me off my throne as the detention king of the family—so long live the queen."

Exasperated, Paige shifted in her seat as the bell rang, thus bringing lunch to a miserable end. In a flash, the boys grabbed their stuff, and stared at Paige one last time. In perfect chorus, they broke out in laughter and bolted toward the instruction halls.

"I should be mad at Preston, but how can I be? This is all my fault," Paige said as the girls tried to comfort her. "What was I thinking? Maybe I should plead temporary insanity like he does when he gets in trouble. Oh, who am I trying to fool—it never works for him either."

After the four of them reached Instructional Hall A, Paige and

Elise sprinted to their Eso-4 class or *flake* studies, as everyone around campus liked to call it. Merely stepping inside the auditorium was always an adventure, for its walls were decorated from ceiling to floor with a menagerie of strange gadgets and tools. Finding themselves amid a game of musical chairs, they rushed to their seats, ducking and weaving past several classmates as Precept Nighswonger called their names from the class roster. Finally reaching the last name on the list, he unlocked a drawer in his desk and pulled out a musty dog-eared book, setting it on his desk with an enormous thud.

"Students—all right, keep it down. Okay, *this* is the first book written and type-set by Heglin Hesselgesser." Writing the name in big bold letters on the board, he turned to his class. "I assume you've all read the first two chapters of our text, Snowflake: Lessons in History. Well, his name appeared several times in these chapters. Now, who can tell me who he was?" Struggling to stay still, Paige rolled her eyes as the room went silent. She knew the answer, but to be branded a know-it-all was a fate worse than death. "No one?" he asked, scanning the blank faces. "Mr. Wickvane? How about you? Your family has a long distinguished history here—this should be an easy one for you."

Oh, no! Of all the people to ask, Paige thought. *He can't even count past his fingers and toes.*

Flanked by two boys from his goon squad, Quinten shrugged as he gazed indifferently at the precept. "Haggle Hessenpester? Yeah—sure, I know him. He's that guy that makes that microwave popcorn—the buttered flavor's my favorite," he said, snickering at the notion. "No, wait, I've got it all wrong. Isn't he the guy that makes those weird vacuum cleaners? Yeah, that's it."

Stewing over his unbelievable nerve, Paige glared at Quinten as she leapt up and blurted out the answer. "Precept Nighswonger?

Heglin Hesselgesser was the very first chancellor at Raydencrafft." From his position a few rows down, Quinten shot daggers at her as she sat back down.

"That's correct," Precept Nighswonger said with a wide smile. "And can anyone tell me what Heglin's greatest achievement was?"

Again, a hush fell over the auditorium. Shaking her head, Paige glanced across the sea of stumped students, fixing her eyes on Quinten. From the devious look on his face, he had to be up to something, she was sure of it. *Oh, crud, why is he raising his hand? He's going to do something rotten – I won't let him do it. If only I could make the little twerp say the right answer. Come on, it's – heading the conservatory's construction effort. That's the answer, you brainless creep. Say – heading the conservatory's construction effort. Say it!*

In grueling slow motion, she watched Quinten's mouth open as the precept called on him, and then the strangest thing happened. "Uh—heading the conservatory's construction effort?" he answered. "What—huh?"

With an expression that matched Quinten's, Precept Nighswonger stood there reeling over the boy's correct answer. "Mr. Wickvane, you *do* know your history after all. Class—you see, even Quinten took the time to learn the text."

Speechless, Quinten fidgeted uneasily in his seat, while his buddies stared suspiciously at him. "But I...I didn't—uh, if you say so I guess."

Realizing she'd just broken the school's cardinal rule about using one's gifts against another student, Paige slowly sank down in her seat and gazed around the room. No one had even a slightest clue of what she'd done, not even Quinten. For the remainder of the class, he spent his time trying to explain himself to his stunned cronies while the precept finished his lecture on the human brain and its relation to applied psychophysics.

"—so it's really a work of brilliance when it comes to how things function in one's brain," he said, glancing up at the wall clock. "Now, since we have only a few more minutes before that annoying bell goes off, let's go over today's homework assignment." Immediately, the entire hall erupted in groans as he put his hand in the air. "Now—now, it's not as bad as it sounds. Just read chapter three and answer the review questions at the end. And remember, take Mr. Wickvane's grand example to heart and—read—read—read. It's the best way to stay ahead of the game."

Trapped in his seat, Quinten threw a weak smile at the mass of students who were gawking at him. Watching him squirm, Paige giggled at his predicament. Suddenly, his eyes locked on her—in that split second, she knew he'd figured it out.

"All right, I need two students to assist me on one last demonstration before we end this session," Precept Nighswonger said eagerly. "I'll need a snowflake and someone from another order." Scanning each row of seats, he frowned as it became apparent that again there were no volunteers. "Miss Brandymire and Mr. Wickvane, would you mind? Since you both were kind enough to help out earlier, I'll make it well worth your trouble—say an extra five credits for each of you."

No—not now, Paige thought as her mind went numb. *Why me? Pick someone else—please.*

Oozing snake-like charm, Quinten jumped from his seat, raring to go. "Sure, I'm game, but only if Paige helps out too." Quickly, he made a beeline towards her, and slithered up next to her with a wily grin on his face. "I know you pulled that mind game on me, you little suck up," he whispered. "You'll regret that." Staring right through her, he prodded her from behind to drive his point home.

"Maybe I'll take it out on your brother's hide, what do you think?"

Paige shot him a sharp glare and gritted her teeth. "You know, you're just a stuck-up creep with bad breath. Besides, you wouldn't want to be around me when I get mad, nothing nice ever comes from it."

Chuckling, he pushed her forward, and put his lips next to her ear. "Oh—no, the puny princess is going to come after me. Oh, I'm so scared."

When they reached the floor of the auditorium, Precept Nighswonger handed Paige a smooth plum-sized stone that glowed as it touched her palm. Ice blue in color, it was almost identical to the Laurelean Bloom she wore.

"Okay, class—Miss Brandymire holds a very rare Chantalean Bloom found in the abandoned mines of Voorhaven. It is one of only a handful to be unearthed since the mines collapsed."

Handing Quinten a gunmetal lockbox, he faced his class and raised a hand to quiet them. "Now, let's get on to the demonstration. Because you are all far too young to have a full understanding of the gifts you possess, your ability to control them will be limited. But, with a gemstone like the one Miss Brandymire is holding, anyone who possesses the abilities of a snowflake will have instantaneous control over them." Excited as a child, he backed away and gazed at Paige. "Miss Brandymire, hold the stone tight in your hand and concentrate on the object Mr. Wickvane is holding," he instructed. "Now, close your eyes and try to imagine the box in your mind, and *will* it to disappear."

Making faces at his friends, Quinten clowned around as he waited impatiently for something to happen—and POOF! He *and* the box vanished, bringing the class to a standstill. As the room went silent, Paige peeked through her fingers to find an empty space where

Quinten once was, and from there, the proceedings took a bizarre turn. "Hey, what's going on? Why's everybody acting so weird?" Quinten's bodiless voice asked. "Somebody say something—why are you all looking at me that way?"

Sputtering, Precept Nighswonger stared nervously at Paige, and then in the direction of Quinten's voice. "Mr. Wickvane—Quinten—try to remain calm. I'm afraid I don't know how to say this, but it seems you've been rendered—invisible."

CLANG! The invisible lockbox hit the floor as Quinten panicked. "You—you did this to me," he screamed at Paige. "Put me back! Now! You little—" In a wild frenzy, he ran at her, tossing chairs to the side as she shot out the doors in tears, running frantically down the hall.

Bolting out the exit, she ran into the park, then stopped and grabbed her hair. *I've messed up everything again. What am I going to do? What if Quinten stays invisible?*

"Paige? Where are you?" Elise called out. "Paige?"

"Elise, I'm over here—in the bushes," she whispered. "Is Quinten okay?"

With a frown, she nodded. "The bell rang, and he popped up out of nowhere. You should've seen it. He was so bent out of shape that when he and his friends finally left, they almost knocked each other's brains out trying to get through the door." Squinting at the park's clock tower, Elise's eyes lit up as she glanced back towards the instruction halls. "Oh, no, we're going to be late!"

Quickly, they weaved through the park, reaching the hall's entrance in record time. "I hope Quinten's not looking for me, you know how he likes to ditch class," Paige said, peering down the length of the hall. "He might be hiding around here."

"Well, I don't see the little cry-baby anywhere," Elise said, smirking. “Ummm, we’d better get going. I’ll see you after class.”

“I’ve got detention, remember?” she said as Elise winced at the thought. “I guess I’ll see you when I’m done.”

Chapter Twenty-Four

Rats, Bullies and Bad Dreams

"Ah, the *liberator* of rats has returned to the scene of the crime," Precept Malineus said in a dreary voice. Rising from behind her desk, she stared coolly at Paige through her icy green eyes. "Miss Brandymire, it is beyond my comprehension why you chose to squander my time with your incredibly childish escapade. It pains me to say just how disappointed I am at your behavior."

Running a hand through her long snow-white hair, she glided over to the cages as her white embroidered overdress flowed behind her. "Well, there they are—your devoted subjects await you," she said, pointing a slender finger at the rats. "Perhaps you'll consider the consequences before attempting something so foolish again."

Paige eyed the cages and started cleaning them one after another, slowly drowning in gloom. Once she'd finished, Precept Malineus shot her a wicked look. "I'll expect you here on Monday. I suggest you use the weekend to reflect on your actions. You may leave now." Giving her a curt wave, she went back to grading papers, leaving Paige fidgeting in place.

"Ummm...uh, thank you, Ma'am," Paige said, backing away as she said each word. Slipping into the hallway, she hurried out the rear exit and snuck between the two buildings. Cautiously, she edged up to the front entrance, peeking around the corner for a sign of Quinten.

"Paige?" Preston asked. "What are you doing? Elise just went in to find you."

Stepping into the open, she gazed unhappily at him. "Did she tell you what happened?"

"Yeah, I'm sorry I missed it." Walking up the steps, he glanced around and peered through the doors. "What's taking her so long? Quinten and his trained apes are bound to show up sooner or later."

Hurrying inside, they found Elise, and shot out the front entrance. "I'm just glad this day's almost over," Paige said as they cut through the park. "You know, I'm beginning to think I should have stayed in bed when the alarm didn't go off this morning."

Elise tried not to laugh as she put her hands on Paige's shoulders. "Yeah, rats and bullies—they're really too much to take in one day, aren't they?" As she was about to reply, Preston groaned, then stopped dead in his tracks.

"I don't believe it," he said, clenching his fists. "It's Quinten."

From the far end of the park, he and his goons cut across their path, stopping in front of them. "Well, if it isn't the chancellor's walking and talking pet project," he shouted, sneering at Paige and Preston. Shifting his icy stare to Elise, he pointed a bony finger at her.

"Why are you still hanging around with these losers? You don't owe them squat."

"Quinten, all you want is an excuse to be mean and nasty," she said, looking Preston's way. "I've never seen things the way you do—and I never will."

Instantly, Quinten's face went red as he shook his fist at her. "Come on, think about it. Everything's different since they showed up. And you want to know something else? They don't even pay their own way. Yeah, you heard me right—they're just a couple of low-rent drop-outs." As Quinten rattled off a string of nasty remarks, his goons circled Preston, then tackled him to the ground.

"Quinten, make them stop!" Elise screamed as he cackled at her.

"Oh, don't worry. I'm just giving him a little taste of what I got from his bratty little sister here." He flashed his steely, brace-filled grin, and grabbed Paige by the arm. "You shouldn't have left before I had a chance to thank you, that wasn't very nice at all." Dragging Paige over to where Preston laid, he flung her into the hands of one of his apes. "I bet you thought that was pretty funny, huh?" he snarled at her. "Well, the next time you try that, this is what you'll get." With pure delight, he raised his foot above Preston, and sent it smashing down on him. Suddenly, a pool of golden light slammed into Quinten and his pals, suspending them in a rippling time rift.

"Preston, we've got to go!" Elise yelled as Paige pulled at him. "Hurry! It won't last, it never does!" Preston stared up at the pitiful Popsicle Quinten had become, and rolled out from under his foot. Taking off at a full run, they all looked back to see Elise's time trap collapse as it released Quinten and his friends from its grasp.

"Was that what I think it was?" Preston shouted at Elise as

they ran to the rec hall. "I saw something like that in Lumenayre's class, but this was way better."

Double timing it, they slipped inside the entrance, and peered out the door. "Preston, do you think he'll come after us?" Paige asked nervously. "I don't see him anywhere, do you?"

Carefully, his eyes searched the area for a sign of them. "Nope, they probably ran for the hills," he said, smiling at Elise. "After what you did, I really can't blame him." Lifting her off the ground, he playfully spun her around, then pulled them both into the gaming room. "Come on, let's turn this day around. Hey, it can't get any worse, because we're not going to let it."

Within the solitude of the park, the clock tower softly clicked and clanked as it kept watch over the campus. Quietly, its bell tolled twice, leaving the tranquil and dreamy peace that had settled over the conservatory unbroken. But if you traveled beyond the park and took a closer look, all was not quiet.

From atop the girl's quarters, Paige stared down from the third floor fire escape. Gathering her nerves, she worked her way down, trying not to make the slightest sound. With a thud, she dropped to the grass, circling around back towards the boy's quarters. As she rounded the corner, Preston walked out from the shadows, backpedaling the second he saw her. "Paige? Holy crud, you almost made me jump out of my skin."

"But, what's going on?" From his expression, she knew he was upset, and in her mind, she knew why. "You had the dream, didn't you?" she asked as her spirits fell. "Preston, what we saw can't be true, can it?"

Putting his hands to his face, Preston took a deep breath. "I don't know what to think, but if it's true, he's the only one standing in her way. Paige, we've got to stop her before *She* finds him. You saw what's going to happen—if we don't, everyone's going to die."

"I know!" Quickly, she pulled off her backpack and unzipped it to show him an assortment of breakfast bars, trail mix and candy. "I thought we might need these. So I crammed everything I could find into it."

Preston pulled on the strap of his backpack. "Yeah, I did too. Ummm, we'd better head to the stables," he said, slipping on his baseball cap. "I saw some camping gear in the storage bins the last time I was there."

Skirting along the edge of the river, they carefully made their way to the stables, staying in the shadows as they went. "Okay, you wait here and I'll find us a horse," Preston said tensely. "Ummm, I'm not all that sure about the saddle part, so this might take awhile."

"Preston?" she asked, shoving her hands into jacket. "Are you sure we're doing the right thing? I mean, what if we're wrong?"

"I hope we're wrong," he said as his voice turned somber, "but if we're not, we've got to stop her."

"Stop who?" Wil asked as he snuck up behind them with Terrin in tow. "Uh, isn't it a little early for a morning ride?"

"Wil? How?" Preston sputtered as Paige gawked at Terrin. "What are you doing out here?"

"Me? Hey, I *always* go for a walk at two in the morning," he said as Preston rolled his eyes at him. "Okay—okay, Terrin called my cel after she followed Paige to the fire escape. So we snuck out to see where you were going."

Preston made a face at Paige and shook his head. "Well, you

can go back right now. This is our problem, not yours, so just forget you ever saw us."

Closing an eye, Wil grinned mischievously at Preston. "No, I think I'll stay. Besides, I wouldn't mind a little fun for a change."

"Fun? You're nuts—it's not like we're going to the mall."

Wil shrugged and smiled devilishly at Preston. "Uh, okay, I *could* tell Thayne about what you're doing. I'm sure he'd want to know, but that's up to you."

"What? You wouldn't—that's blackmail!" Preston said, staring narrowly at him.

Smirking, Wil patted him on the shoulder. "Blackmail? I kinda like to think of it as a friend helping a friend."

"Excuse me! I hate to ruin your little party, but what about me?" Terrin asked. "I'm not walking back to my chamber alone. Somebody's got to take me back, it's either that or I scream bloody murder."

"Oh, come on, we're going the other way," Preston said, pointing towards the woods. Turning red, he glared at Wil. "You brought her, you take her back." In a defiant last stand, Wil and Terrin stood there in silence as Preston peered at them from under his cap. "Fine, do whatever you want, but we're leaving."

Wil and Terrin gawked at each other, then ran into the stables. Throwing his hands up, Preston frowned at Paige as Wil reappeared with two horses trailing behind him. "Great," Preston said as he pointed at Terrin, "come if you want, but I'm not chasing after you if you can't steer a horse."

Once they were a safe distance away, Preston stopped and gazed at the moonlit conservatory one last time. "I didn't think I'd ever say this, but I'm going to miss this place. I just wish I could have said goodbye to Elise."

Shivering, Paige bundled herself up and smiled. "If you would have told her, she would've wanted to come, so it's better that she doesn't know."

Preston gave her a somber nod and stared up at the stars as he turned away from the conservatory and thoughts of Elise. Gripping his colt's reins, he tried to ignore the giant lump in his stomach. *What am I doing? I don't have a clue of where we're going or how we're going to stop her.* Steadfast, he fought back his doubts, then led them away from Raydencrafft, down a lonely path toward the unknown.

Chapter Twenty-Five

The Forest Keeper

"My butt hurts," Terrin whined, wiggling around in the saddle, "and I'm getting really tired. When are we going to stop?"

Rolling his eyes, Preston pulled back on the reins and glared at her. "Are you finished?" he snapped as his horse whinnied in agreement. "Keep it up and you'll be walking back to school. It's just a few days back that way, but that's if you run *real* fast."

"Hey, don't blame me," she grumbled. "Sitting on this saddle's like sitting on a pile of rocks. Paige, tell them I'm right."

"Oh, no, I'm not getting in the middle of this, uh-uh. I've got bigger things to worry about, like *not* falling off this horse."

With a grunt, Terrin shoved her forward as they continued along the path, zigzagging through the growing obstacle course of gnarled branches.

"Uh, I hate to say this, but it's really getting dark in here," Wil said, gazing down the length of the trail. "Isn't it almost noon? Where'd the sun go?" Staring up at the thick canopy of trees, he lit his hand in red fire only seconds before a limb whipped around and slammed into him, sending him crashing to the ground.

"Wil!" Preston yelled, jumping down to him. "Geez, are you okay?"

"Oh—owww!" he groaned as the girls gawked at him. "Man, that hurt!"

Struggling to his feet, Wil's mouth fell open as he looked over Preston's shoulder. "Whoa! What's that?" Quickly, they all turned around. "Uh, tell me I've cracked my head open—that can't be real, can it?" Before they could answer, he scrambled down the ivy covered embankment, sliding to a stop near the steps of an enormous stone temple. "Look at this place—I bet it's full of booby-traps," he said, peeking around the side of the shrine. "I think I'll— "

CRASH! CLANG! "Holy crud, something's in there!" Wil shouted as everyone stopped dead in their tracks.

Waving the girls back, Preston walked up next to him and peered inside. "I can't see a thing," he whispered as something scurried around in the shadows. "Hey, you'd better come out!"

CLANK! THUD! And then silence. "That's it, I'm tossing in a vapor sphere," Wil said, glancing uneasily at Preston. "Whoever's in there, let's see if you like this!" Out of his wind-up, he let loose a fireball straight at the entrance, and immediately, the panicked voice of a child bellowed out.

"I mean you no harm—no harm. Please hurt me not—no hurt. Surrender I do," the jittery voice said. "Come out I will, promise I do." From the doorway, a small, girlish-looking boy emerged waving his hands in the air. He resembled a flawless porcelain doll with skin as white as alabaster, and wore nothing but tattered animal skins garlanded in colored feathers and leaves.

"But he—he's just a boy," Paige said as Terrin studied him keenly. "Ummm, what are you doing out here? It's the middle of nowhere."

Cocking his head, the boy stared crossly at her. "A *boy* you say? Look like one I might, but surely not am I—for a woodland sprite am I," he explained, his coal black eyes focusing on Preston and Wil. "Much longer have I been in this forest than you, little one. But for you to call my home *nowhere,* offends me it does. The forest dark is hardly *nowhere* – it is here, is it not?"

"I'm sorry, I didn't mean for it to come out that way," she said with a smile. "But—ummm, a sprite, I've never heard of it. What's it mean?"

Scrunching his nose, the boy mulled over her question as if he wasn't any surer of it than she was. "Mean? *Me* it means," he answered plainly. "For a wood faerie by any other name am I, and the forest, my keep."

"A fairy?" she asked. "Wait a minute, aren't you supposed to have wings?"

Annoyed, he raised a brow. "Wings? Need them not do I—many ways to fly there are—yes?"

Paige shrugged off his answer, choosing to drop the issue instead. "So, my name's Paige, what's yours?"

Smirking at them, he tapped his finger against his chin. "Ummm, my name? Long it is—say it, you could not. Cail, you try, yes? Much shorter—easier to say. Cail it is."

Curiously, the sprite gazed at Preston and Paige. "A kinship you have, do you not? You seek the Anfiora as *She* does, yes? Destroy it *She* will, find it first *She* must." Staring up at the trees, Cail's face went sullen. "Cunning *She* is. Much pain does the forest feel when her way is had—dark days it has suffered at her whim, very dark days."

"But how could you know this?" Preston said, glancing nervously at Paige. "We've never seen you before."

"True this is, seen you before—no. The forest, tells me of your plight it does. Perilous is the road upon which you tread," he said, motioning to the entrance. "Yet to come are the days that worrisome things such as these will befall us. Sacred is this shrine, protected by the forest spirits it is. Stay here for the night you will—to you, no harm shall come."

Skipping up the steps, Cail guided them into the temple, then flicked his wrist to launch a shower of fiery sparks from his fingertips. Out of the shadows, a string of torches ignited, casting their golden glow on the marble sprites that stood silent sentry around the anteroom. In the center, seven massive stone columns rose up to the ceiling forming a large circular hub. Separated into seven slices, the floor had gold inlays identical to the orders at Raydencrafft, right up to the crescent moon that sat in its marble heart.

As they walked into the center of the marble hub, Wil's eyes widened. "Preston—our marks, they're glowing," he said as a rainbow of light sprang from them. "What's going on, what *is* this place?"

Skirting along the outer edge, Cail poked his head between the columns and threw them an impish grin. "Outlanders you are—very good this is. The forest spirits, like you they do." Enveloped in a sudden cloud of gloom, he gazed somberly at them. "To this shrine many of your kin once journeyed. Many summers ago *She* too would come, but now, a different path *She* follows. Visit here no one does anymore—brought you the spirits have—wise they are."

Preston made a face at Wil, then threw Cail a weak smile.

"Okaaay, but maybe we should get our things inside and eat something. Is it all right if we sleep over there?"

Beaming from ear to ear, Cail nodded and began chattering as he hurried towards another room. "Food—sleep. Earthly needs, forgotten them I have. Remedy that I will, promise I do."

After laying out their sleeping bags, they sat down in a circle, and nibbled on a couple of bags of pretzels as Cail re-emerged. Carrying a large bowl in one hand and a reddish lava rock in the other, he scurried over to them and planted himself between Preston and Paige. "Promised I did—bring you something good. Never do we wood sprites need to eat, but eat these we do. Treats of pleasure they are."

Putting a bowl of roasted *nuts* in front of him, Cail popped one into his mouth, and rolled it around on his tongue. "Prickly pebbles from a woe bush they are—very rare. Whilst you travel, keep you full they will. A long time will they last," he said, sliding the bowl over to Wil and Terrin. "Take one, good they are."

Terrin picked one up and touched it to her tongue, grinning as she stuck it in her mouth. "Hey, he's right, they taste great," she exclaimed, chewing away like a chipmunk. "Come on, you guys have to try them." With her stamp of approval, they each dropped a pebble in their mouths, happily sucking on them like hard candy.

Fidgeting at the success of his sweets, Cail set the stone in the center of their circle. "Eat this not you do. Rosestone of ash this is, from An'nonne Duerre it came. Never need heat us sprites do, for you this is," he said, waving his hands over it. Instantly, the stone sparkled and glowed as a warm aura filled the air around them. "A gift for your journey, enchanted it is. Speak my name, and keep you warm it will."

Happily, Cail began to rattle off one tall-tale after another while Preston and the others basked in the warmth of the Rosestone. As they began to doze off, the faerie doused the torches, one by one, bringing the day to a peaceful end.

Chapter Twenty-Six

Journey to RaVyena

"I sure wish Cail could have come with us," Paige said, stroking her mare as they snaked their way through the overgrowth.

Terrin giggled. "Yeah, me too, he was really funny. But I still wonder why he didn't want to come."

"He must have had his reasons. Anyway, who could blame him, that stone motel of his was nice," Preston said as Wil smirked at him. "All it really needs is a TV and some video games."

"You forgot to mention a wall socket," Wil said, leaning forward in his saddle. "By the way, just how far is this bridge Cail told us about? Honestly, I'm starting to wonder if he made it all up."

Giving him a crooked scowl, Preston shrugged. "Don't ask me—white crows and shadowy groves, that's all I got from him," he said, pulling his baseball cap down around his eyes. "But you know what's weird? I've had this strange feeling that we're going the right way ever since we started. Just don't ask me for directions, because I don't have a clue."

Slowly, hours turned to days, and still, Cail's bridge was nowhere in sight. Worries weighed heavily on their minds and mutiny poisoned the air. But inside the claustrophobic menagerie of the dark forest, Preston shuddered at the notion that something horrible laid waiting for them.

Bleak and out-of-the-way, Whitecrow Bridge was the only point for miles where one could cross the white waters of the Blackenville River. A short distance away, Shadowens Grove stood silent guard over the decaying bridge, waiting for those who were reckless enough to cross it.

Hidden within the grove, two dark-stars watched the approach to the bridge. Stealing through the thicket, they trained their twisted minds on the thoughts of any and all unsuspecting travelers. Suddenly, one of them held up her hand. *"Someone approaches,"* she said telepathically to the other. *"A strange sensation runs down my spine – we must wait."*

Fixing their eyes on the trail, the pair inched closer, pausing to stare down its length. In the distance, the sound of horse hooves echoed through the woods. Like statues of stone, the dark-stars stood motionless, sighting what had, at last, strayed into their trap.

Questioning the weird compass he'd been relying upon, Preston wiped the sweat from his forehead as he strained to see as far forward as he could. The others were well beyond restless, yet he hardly could blame them, for they'd seen nothing but miles of rotten forest so far. All hope had seemed lost, when the sound of rushing water and a hint of daylight broke through the trees.

"See—the river," Preston announced triumphantly, "I told you we were going the right way."

Wil reached the bridge first, then jumped down from his horse and glanced over the edge at the raging waters below. "Whoa! That's a long ways down." Carefully, he took a few steps onto the wood deck and shot a nervous look at Preston. "Oh, man, tell me I'm not seeing this. This bridge is a total wreck," he said as each board groaned under his weight. "I don't know about you, but I'm not too crazy about taking a white water trip without a raft today."

Preston stepped firmly onto the first wooden plank, jumping back as it creaked. "Uh, we'd better be careful. We'll check each board first when we walk the horses across."

As they crossed the expanse, the girls held on to each other while they stared down at the torrent of water. "Terrin!" Paige yelled as a section of planks broke away from under them. Instantly, Terrin fell through the opening, screaming as she dangled above the watery abyss.

"Preston! Grab her!" Wil shouted. "Hurry!"

Diving for her, Preston pulled the hysterical girl up through the gap, and guided her over to Paige as he scowled at Wil. "This rotten woodpile's falling apart around us—we'll never make it across!" With no other choice before them, they slowed to a crawl, carefully leading the horses around the gaping hole as Paige tried to calm Terrin along the way.

"Don't worry, we're almost off this thing," Preston said as he gazed at the horizon. "No! Not here—not now!" From above the woods, four shifters swooped down towards them, landing at the far end of the bridge. Sprouting snake-like tentacles, they closed in as Preston and Wil pulled the horses in the other direction. "Go back! We've got to get off this bridge! Run!" Instantly, they backpedaled to a stop as four dark-dwellers emerged from the grove, blocking their way.

Ensnared in an all-out ambush, Preston frantically searched for an escape as he watched Demora's followers tighten their net around them. Grabbing Paige, he held her tight, realizing they had nowhere to run.

Chapter Twenty-Seven

Quagmire

Whitecrow Bridge was dying. Like whale song, the bridge's groaning death throws echoed across the sea of evergreens. From atop its crumbling deck, Preston clenched his fists as he glared at the darkshifters who were fast approaching. "If they expect me to just put my hands up, they're in for a big surprise. I swear, I'm going down swinging before that happens."

Staring shrewdly at their horses, he threw Wil a crafty smile as he ran behind them. "Guys—move out of the way." With a firm slap, he drove the horses forward. "Eat that, you tunnel happy freaks!" Swiftly, the rampaging steeds tore at the rotting bridge as they collided head-on with one of the shifters, launching him over the side. In a surreal blur, he vanished into the rapids as his companions fixed their glowing indigo eyes on Preston.

"You little cuss, you've run out of horses to throw at us," the leader snarled. "I'm now of a mind to toss one of you in after him to even the score!" Closing in on them, he and his companions spread out, when from out of the horizon, an enormous ball of fiery red plasma slammed into them. Instantly, the explosion took out the side of the bridge, engulfing the three in flames as they plunged into the swirling torrent below.

"Run!" Preston shouted as Paige grabbed Terrin and pulled at her. Instead, the girl broke away from her and started walking back toward the grove as Wil followed close behind. "What are you guys doing? It's the other way!" Without uttering a word, they looked right through Preston as he blocked their way. "Paige! Something's wrong!" Struggling to hang onto them, he glanced in the direction of Shadowens Grove, focusing on the two women standing at the bridge's edge. "They're stars—they're making them do this!"

Dragging Terrin and Wil to the center of the bridge, Preston turned as another fireball came roaring down, knocking the dark-stars to the ground. In chorus, the two kids snapped out of their trance, and gazed incredulously at each other. "Wil! Terrin! We've got to go," Preston barked as he grabbed them. "Come on, we're running out of time."

All around them, massive wooden beams fell like dominos into the raging waters as Preston and Wil scrambled through the moving obstacle course dragging Paige and Terrin behind them.

"Preston," Wil yelled as they reached the other side, "they're coming!"

From the opposite end of the bridge, two dark-dwellers raced across the span, but before they could make it halfway, they were hit by another crimson blast that sent them over the side. Scanning the skyline, Preston finally saw the source of the aerial attack—a man rid-ing an enormous reptilian bird of prey. Keenly, he followed the giant bird across the horizon, unaware that Wil was pointing frantically at the bridge.

"Preston! Watch out!" Wil yelled as a wave of energy plowed into them. Sent spinning like a top, they somersaulted into the girls only to be caught within a surging containment web. Seconds later, the last of Demora's followers reached the center of the bridge, then bolted toward them as a woman on horseback charged from the grove onto the bridge. Bounding through the debris, she galloped towards the two attackers as they wheeled around to face her. Swiftly, the dark-wave reared back to launch an attack, but was struck by yet another devastating barrage that hurled him off the bridge in a ball of flame.

Flying past the stunned dark-star, the woman dodged and weaved through the wreckage, making a final push to escape the carnage. One last mournful groan rumbled through Whitecrow Bridge as it collapsed upon itself, swallowing the dark-star with it.

All at once, the web surrounding Preston and the others faded away, leaving them staring up at the regal woman as she jumped off her snow white stallion. "Precept Malineus?" Paige exclaimed. "But how did—oh, we're in trouble now." Helping them to their feet, she glared at the tongue-tied girl in astonishment.

"Trouble? Miss Brandymire, you've an exceptional way of understating the obvious," she said, shaking her head. "I can only hope that you realize how much trouble you've caused by traipsing through this forest—it was dangerously irresponsible."

Above Shadowens Grove, the giant winged reptile reappeared as it flew over the chasm and the river below. When it landed, Preston's mouth fell open as he saw the man sitting atop the scaly creature. "Oh, geez, it's Precept Dryden. Holy crud, now we're really in trouble."

Jumping down, Samiel scowled at Preston, then backed away as the bird morphed into Pete Jeffries. "What in the world were you thinking?" he said bluntly. "Demora's dark-seekers are lurking in every corner of this forest searching for the same thing you are." Taken by surprise, Preston sputtered as Samiel went on. "Yes, that's right, thanks to you and the maps you found, we know about the Anfiora vial as well as Damon's plan to transfer his life-force into it." Running a hand through his blond hair, he glanced at Pete and looked out over the gorge. "We need to round up their horses. Do you think you'll be able to carry them across the chasm?"

With a calculating stare, Pete gauged the distance and nodded. "Sure, it might take some time, but it won't be a problem."

Preston's eyes lit up as he shot daggers at the two of them. "Hold on, what are you talking about?" he shouted. "We can't go back."

"Preston, the chancellor's orders were clear about this. He doesn't want you, or any other student, put in danger."

"Precept Dryden—sir—I'm sorry, but you haven't seen what's about to come our way," he said tensely. "So take Wil and Terrin back, but Paige and I have to finish this before *She* finishes us." Kicking up a cloud of dirt, he stomped down the path, and swung back around to face them. "You know, I never asked to be a rotten crescent. I didn't have a choice. But I know I have to do this even if it kills me. Besides, nobody's going to miss us anyway. There'll just be two less charity-case crescents to talk about."

"Charity cases? That's ridiculous. But if what you've said is true, we have as much of a responsibility to save Damon as you do," Samiel said. "So we have two choices—turn back or keep going. Either way, Pete will have to take Mr. Buller and Miss Matthews back to

Raydencrafft."

Defiantly, Wil shook his head and stepped up next to Preston as Terrin followed suit. Focusing her cool pale gaze on them, Precept Malineus frowned as she tapped her finger against her lips. "I hope you realize what this trip will actually involve. The vial's hidden somewhere in the area surrounding the peaks of Ravyena—the way there is plagued by very rough terrain, and to compound the problem, the dark-seekers you just met won't be the last we'll see. So, I'm asking you once again, are you sure you won't change your minds?"

Undaunted, they gave her a quick nod, and peered nervously down the bleak path as Samiel glanced at the setting sun. "We should stay here for the night," he said, climbing onto his gray mount. "Pete, get them started on setting up camp. I'll track down their horses." Pulling back on the reins, he swung his horse around, then disappeared down the trail.

"Hey, this place is way better than that black hole we just came from," Wil said as he and Preston carried rocks over to a makeshift fire pit. "At least we can see the sky, and if you ask me, that's a real big plus."

The last bit of sunshine filtered through the trees as Samiel rode up the path, towing the missing horses behind him. A boy lay over his saddle like a rice sack, chattering as he struggled to free himself. "To you I explained—try I do, help you I will."

"Cail?" Preston shouted as he ran up to them. "But I...uh, what are you doing here?"

"Preston, don't tell me you know this boy?" Samiel asked, lifting Cail down off the saddle. "He was trailing me the entire time, and I've just spent the last hour chasing him down."

"Boy? A wood sprite am I," Cail announced, brushing himself off. "Difficult it is to tell the difference, only one so *old* as you would have this much trouble seeing it."

"Cail, what's going on? You told us you couldn't leave," Preston asked. "How did you get here? The bridge is gone."

"To journey through the forest dark, a bridge I need not. To come and help, changed my mind I did," he said, glaring resentfully at Samiel. "Know the forest I do. Show you the way I will. But listen to reason, yellow-haired old man would not, refused he did."

"Okay Preston, if you want him to come, he's your problem," Samiel said heatedly. "But if he slows us down, he'll find himself walking back to wherever he came from."

Hearing the news, Cail skipped merrily around the fire, the light dancing off his feathered clothing. "Ravyena—the mountain twins," he exclaimed, "take you there I will, help you, yes."

So, as the reluctant heroes spent their first night together, hope sprang eternal within the safety of their growing fellowship. The next morning, they resumed their quest with a newfound energy as Cail led the way.

Chapter Twenty-Eight

The Pit and the Pillar

One after another, the days melded together, until, at last, they reached Ravyena. With a mix of exhilaration and fear, they all gazed uneasily toward the horizon. Through the dense fog, the twin summits rose up over the tree line, looming in the distance like huge stone arrowheads.

"Well, there they are," Samiel said, glancing at Paige and Preston. "Like it or not, we're here."

"Told you I did—show you the way I would," Cail said proudly as his voice turned serious. "This place, full of treachery it is. Many paths one may choose—bear fruit some do, disaster will others bring."

Paige bit her lip and stared at Samiel. "We're so close—will we be able to make it there before dark? I just want to find what we're searching for and go back to school, if they even let us come back."

Silently, Samiel mulled over her question, but before he could say a word, Cail blurted out an answer for him. "Before the eve falls, reach the twins we can," he said eagerly. "Cut the way short I can, be there soon we will."

Pete shook his head and frowned at the wood sprite. "I don't see any reason to rush in there. I think we should scout the area first. Demora might be waiting for us to blunder into one of her traps."

Shying away from the mere mention of Demora, Cail threw a narrow look at Pete. "Rush? Many traps *She* will set, yes? But seldom traveled is the way that is shortest—through the forest it is—no trail by which to follow."

"Uh, I'm not so sure if that's such a good idea," Samiel countered as the faerie fidgeted in place. "Without a clear path, we could easily get lost."

Angrily, the wood sprite sneered at Samiel as Preston scowled at them both. "I don't want to wait any more," he said as Paige gazed fretfully at Samiel. "We need to get there now."

"Preston's right," Paige said softly, "we can't wait any longer."

Samiel closed his eyes and sighed. "Okay, we'll do it the sprite's way—better to get lost than waylaid before we get there."

Breaking from the trail, they followed Cail blindly through a tangled maze of trees, reaching the foothills well before sunset. "Promised you I did. Traps, there are not. Not here is *She.* Find now what you seek, yes? Help you I will."

Paying no attention to the faerie's unending babble, Paige stared up at the rocky hillside and then at Preston. "Preston—this place," she said, putting her hand to her mouth. "It's right out of our dreams."

"Yeah, it is," he said, pulling his cap down. "Oh, man, this can't be good. It's all we need right now, another bunch of rotten tunnels to get lost in."

Completely at a loss, Samiel did a one-eighty. "Okay, stop right there," he demanded as the siblings clammed up. "Good, now tell me what you're talking about."

Leaving nothing to the imagination, they described their dreams, and then Preston wound things down to a finish. "—and I got hit by a humongous ball of blue fire free of charge from her glowingness," he said, slapping his hands together. "KA-POW! Right into the pit I went—and then KER-SPLAT! And that was that." After finishing his quick re-enactment, he shrugged at Wil and Terrin, who looked as white as sheets. "What? It's just a stupid dream. Sure—yeah, some of them might come true, but I'm pretty sure this one's not going to, because if it does, then I'm dead meat."

Springing over the rocks, Cail skipped along the path and came to a stop. With a sly grin, he balanced precariously on an overhanging rock, peering over the edge at Preston. "Dreams and dark tunnels, a molehill's difference they make not. These passageways—know them I do, show you I will."

Samiel surveyed the area and threw Precept Malineus an uneasy glance. "Elex, I don't know, this doesn't feel right," he said, helping the girls down. "It's quiet out here—too quiet."

Jumping down from his perch, Cail smiled coyly at Samiel as he pointed to an opening farther up the mountainside. "Cast off this way has become—lost within one can get, if one knows not the way. Show you the way I will, yes?"

Carefully eyeing the wood sprite, Samiel shook his head. "I don't have much of a say in this, do I? Faerie boy, you better be right."

As they reached the entrance, Cail pointed into the shadows and winked at Samiel. "Light the way must the fire-maker do. A thorny road lies ahead. Prick one's self one must not, yes?"

Journeying forward, they moved cautiously through the innards of the mountain twins, when they came across the unexpected—a stone cold dead-end. "Where did this come from?" Samiel said, reaching out to touch the stone barrier.

"Wait," Preston shouted as he tried to grab him, "don't touch it!" Before he could stop him, they were both hit by a lightning fast burst of energy, and sent flying backwards. Hitting the floor, they gawked at each other.

"What the—?" Samiel said, trying to get his wits about him. "There's a plasma field protecting it!" Getting to his feet, he pulled Preston up, and gazed at the fading shield. "I hate to say this, but without some sort of a miracle, we don't stand a snowball's chance in Hades of making it past this barrier." Waving his flaming hand around, Samiel scowled at Cail. "What is this? I thought you knew these tunnels!"

"Blame me not—trickery this is," the wood sprite said as he rubbed his hands across the rock walls. "Look! In the stone—a crescent moon! Look—look!" Carved into the passageway was the symbol of a crescent, and beside it, the figure of a man. "The boy crescent—within him the answer lies."

Hearing Cail's suggestion, Paige stared anxiously at Preston, then glared at the wood faerie. "What? Cail, you can't be right. In my dream, this was open when I came through here."

Preston smirked as he glanced at Paige. "Ummm, it wasn't when I got here, I opened it," he said as their faces went blank. "Hey, I had that dream a long time ago. Geez, I forgot all about it, that's all."

Samiel slapped his forehead and sighed. "Preston, fine, how do we open it?"

Uneasily, Preston shuffled in place and shrugged. "Well—uh, that's just the thing, it sort of opened by itself."

"Preston!" Paige said, jabbing him in the side. "Why is it that you never have a clue of what's going on?"

Scratching the side of his head, he pleaded the fifth as Samiel took another turn at trying to pry an answer out of him. "Preston, you have to remember something," he said, motioning at the barrier. "What did you do when you got here?"

Preston stepped up to the barrier and rummaged through his pockets, finally producing his Laurelean Bloom amid a clump of pocket lint. "I don't know—it was dark in here, so I used this and WOOSH—the wall disappeared." He waved the glowing stone across the rock surface and backed away, but the barrier remained intact. "Hey, that's not the way it happened," Preston said as he eyed the bloom and shook it. "Uh, maybe the batteries are going dead on this thing." Suddenly, the bloom burst into flames as beams of brilliant light cut through the energy field, bringing the wall down with a booming crash.

Cracking an eye open, Preston peered through the new opening, then glanced at the others. "Whoa, it worked—uh, I think we'd better go before it changes its mind."

Cautiously, they moved through the weaving maze, stopping as they came across a series of wall etchings. Dancing circles around the girls, Cail pointed to the walls. "Writings of the forest elders, sacred they are. Look—look!" he exclaimed, running his hands over them. "Must see more—see more!" Bolting down the path, he disappeared, leaving everyone standing there in shock.

"Cail!" Preston yelled, dashing through the tunnel after him. "Cail—stop!"

Down the path, they could hear the faerie chirp on, but as they closed in on him, it went eerily quiet. Quickly, they spirited through the passage only to end up in a massive circular antechamber. Inside, Cail skipped around the outer ring, humming to himself along the way. "Cail, what the heck are you doing?" Preston asked, screeching to a halt. "Wait a minute, I remember this place. This is where I got dumped into that—hey, where's the pit of death?"

Adorned with bands of carved symbols, the temple had a huge mosaic crescent in the center of the floor as well as the ceiling. Several recessed medallions were set into the walls around the room, each marking an entrance to a tunnel below them. "Shrine of the elders this is," Cail explained as he skipped around them. "A powerful place—strong it is, feel it I do."

Samiel gave Pete and Elex a curious glance and turned to Preston. "So what are we supposed to do? Wander down each of these tunnels until we find the vial?"

"The vial—hidden it is, yes?" Cail asked, giggling softly. "Find it we must—a long time has it been lost." Preston frowned as he and Paige stepped onto the mosaic crescent. Abruptly, the room went dark, and then came a thunderous rumble as each opening slammed shut.

"What's happening? I can't see!" Terrin cried out as she ran head first into Paige. "What are we going to do?"

"Everyone stay calm!" Samiel shouted over Terrin's hysterics. "Pete! Elex! Something's wrong—I can't produce fire—nothing!"

Holding on to Elex, Pete struggled as he tried to morph. "I can't shift either."

As everyone fumbled about, Cail danced around them, giggling like a schoolgirl. "The elders—trapped us they have—nowhere to go, nowhere to run!"

"Cail! Shut up," Samiel barked. "Be quiet, I have to think this through."

"Precept Dryden—look!" Preston blurted out as two glowing pedestals rose up from the floor. Lighting the chamber in emerald green, they each bore symbols identical to those on the stone vault he and Paige had opened in the conservatory's past.

"Through the power of the two will the way become clear," a faceless voice boomed. "Only then can you proceed."

Cail sprang to Preston's side, skipping around him in a mad frenzy. "Yes—yes! The ciphers—kin of the crescent clan must touch, open the path it will."

Staring skeptically at Cail, Samiel waved Paige and Preston over to the panels. "Faerie, for our sakes, I hope you're right. Okay—Preston, when I count to three, you and Paige place your hands on the panels," he instructed. "One—two—three." Together, they touched the gleaming symbols and waited for something—anything—to happen.

With a sudden jolt, tremors rocked the anteroom as the mosaic crescents on the floor and ceiling flickered. Then, amid a sparkling burst of light, the floor's mosaic fell away as a pulsing column of green magma smashed through the ceiling. "The way has been opened," the voice echoed again. "Through the emerald veil you must pass."

Awestruck, they peered into the swirling pillar as Preston shook his head and spoke up. "We're supposed to walk into that? What if it winds up going nowhere?" Taking a deep breath, he walked up to the surging magma and slid his hand into the ooze, pulling it out without a scratch. "Uh, well, I guess I'll see you guys on the other side," he said resignedly as he looked at Paige. "Sis, it'll be all right, you'll see."

Closing his eyes, he vanished into the swirling goo, and then, one by one, they followed him into the emerald twilight.

Chapter Twenty-Nine

In the Lair of the Crescent Moon

Thrashing through the soupy mist, Preston finally emerged on the other side, dropping to his knees as he gazed up at the cavernous columned hall. All around him, huge pools of green magma bubbled and spewed, casting an eerie pallor across the walls. At the far end of the hall, a massive stone relief loomed over him. Covered with hundreds of intricate sculptures and symbols, it traveled up the wall well beyond his view.

Behind him, the molten column began to gurgle as the others slid out from the shimmering ooze. But, as Cail slipped through the glowing gel, he hit the ground running. Darting wildly around the room, he skidded to a stop as if he'd seen a ghost. Motionless, he stood in the center of a circle of seven granite pillars, and stared up at the carved relief. "Close we are. The symbols—in them the answer lies, feel it I do."

Preston scowled and shook his head. "Cail, it's just a bunch of dumb carvings, there's nothing here."

"Dumb? Folly you mean? No—the symbols, tell a story they do," he explained as he led Paige and Preston into the ring of pillars. "Lead to what we seek they do." As they stepped into the center, each of the pedestal heads exploded in a blast of blinding light. Chattering feverishly, the faerie ran for cover as huge spheres of white formed over each stone pillar, then hovered and spun like tops.

"Don't move," Samiel warned, running toward them. "Stay put. Wait—right—there." Huddling together, Paige and Preston covered their faces as a brilliant explosion of fireworks shot from the swirling globes, creating a gigantic pulsing orb of emerald green. Suddenly, bolts of light erupted from the flickering sphere, causing a large section of the wall to fall away, revealing a hidden passageway.

"Told you I did, find the way we would," the sprite said, dancing around Samiel. "Believe me now, yes?"

Samiel wheeled around to look the wood faerie straight in the eyes. "Okay, I believe you, but next time, you might want to grab the kids as you're running for the hills, you got me?"

Without a word, Cail wrinkled his nose and skipped sheepishly away with Pete watching him like a hawk. "I hate to say it, but the faerie boy's wearing out his welcome. He's been an annoying second shadow ever since we got here."

Nodding, Samiel stepped inside the doorway as Preston and Pete peered in behind him. Bit by bit, their vision adjusted to the gloom, revealing a shocking reality. Where a floor should have been, only a narrow stone pathway stood in its place. Far below, a vast ocean of molten lava sat at the bottom of a sheer mind-numbing drop.

Overpowered by the thick stench of volcanic sulfur, Samiel

hastily retreated. "There's barely enough space to walk in there—and nothing to keep us from falling. I'm sorry, but we can't go any farther, we're finished here."

"No! To stop me the yellow-haired man wishes! No!" Cail screamed as he bolted through the opening. "Find it first, I must!"

"Oh, crud—not again!" Preston yelled. "Cail! Stop!" Running after him, he skirted across the razor's edge of stone, when, finally, he saw what Cail was heading for—an enormous circular stone platform. Shaped much like an aviary, huge stone arches swept over it, forming a dome. Below the apex of the arches, a shimmering object floated in midair. *It's the vial! And there's Cail—but what's he doing?* From his vantage point, Preston watched the faerie leap up at the vial as if trying to strike it. But as Cail did, a blazing bolt of energy struck him, sending the faerie flying backwards.

"Cail? What are you doing?" Preston shouted. "Are you crazy?"

"Crazy? Like a hatter? No—help you I tried—led you here, yes?" he countered, pointing up at the radiant energy globe. "Tried to reach it, but defended it is, misguided I was." As his uncertainty grew, Preston eyed Cail, then gazed up at the very object that had plagued his dreams for months. Surrounded by a pulsating plasma sphere, the glass cylinder twirled end over end as a swirling storm of emerald vapor sparkled inside it.

"Preston! Cail!" Samiel yelled as he reached them. "I can't believe you just did that!" With a sputter of desperation, Preston tried to spit out some kind of explanation as the others came running down the stone pathway.

Reaching the platform next, Pete grabbed Paige and Wil as they came within arms reach, then waited for Elex, who was guiding a sobbing Terrin. Furious, he shook his fist at Cail. "I don't know what you're up to, but that's the last time you'll get a chance to do that," he thundered, pointing down to the fiery abyss. "I'm warning you, just sneeze the wrong way and you'll have to sprout wings to save yourself."

Slipping in between them, Samiel held Pete back as Cail cowered behind Preston. "Enough! What's done is done," he said sternly, glancing up at the vial. "Right now, we need to focus."

"You're right," Pete conceded. "We're here, so let's finish this before something does happen."

Samiel nodded and walked to the center of the platform. "Keep away from the edge and stay put." He looked down at Cail, who was acting as jittery as a caged cat. "*That* goes especially for you." For a moment, his eyes lingered on the sprite, then darted to the ring of gold inlayed symbols at his feet. "These inlays, I think they have something to do with freeing the vial."

Again, the faceless voice boomed. "The two halves of the key must be put in place—for the lock has been set in motion." Instantly, streams of emerald magma flowed from the apex above the Anfiora, down into the deep crevices of the arches. Seeping into the platform, the lava swirled below the surface, forming two sparkling circles on opposite sides connected by a pulsating band of green.

"Yes—yes," Cail howled as he ran circles around Paige and Preston, "step into the glowing rings you must."

"Great! That figures," Preston said as he stared at Paige. "Don't worry, it'll be over soon, I promise." Tearfully, she walked to the other side of the platform and gazed at him, and then they each stepped into the center of the rings.

"The key is one," the voice roared. "The power of the two is complete."

Amid a surge of light, the band between them went white-hot

as a blazing arrow of pure energy shot up at the Anfiora's shield, piercing its flaming heart. Inch by inch, the emerald beam pulled the plasma sphere down, finally triggering the shield's demise as the vial came to rest.

"Is it over?" Paige asked, cracking open her eyes. "Preston—is it?"

"Uh, yeah, I think so."

"Then, can we go now?" she asked. Preston turned and made a face at her as he edged closer to the cylinder. Suddenly, Cail darted past them and snatched up the vial, then dashed to the far end of the platform.

"Mine, the vial is!" he shouted, shaking a fist at them. "Come near—and harm you I will—"

Chapter Thirty

End Game

Grasping the Anfiora in one hand, Cail hissed at them as Pete broke ranks and ran at him. Shrouded in a flickering blue aura, he hit Pete with a rippling wave of energy and sent him spiraling backwards into one of the arches. Hands blazing, Samiel moved towards Cail as the faerie threw him a devilish smile. "To harm me you wish—yes?" he asked, glancing down at Pete, lying unconscious on the rock floor. "Your distance you will keep—or yours will his fate be."

"Cail? Why?" Terrin sputtered as Paige held her back. "We're your friends, you can't do this."

Giggling, his eyes began to glow indigo. "*Friends?* Yes. *Help* you I will—*yes?*" he mused as his tone changed. "Your gullibility amuses me." Twirling the vial like a worthless toy, he teetered it on his fingertips and sneered at them. "That absurd faerie of yours was no better. The little pest had set out to warn you of my plans when I crossed his path. But since I hold no grudges, I've seen fit to let him spend the rest of his days in that ridiculous shrine of his, sealed away for an eternity as I was."

At hearing the wood sprite's fate, Preston moved past Terrin and glared at him. "Boy, what does it matter? In your present predicament, you can hardly lift a finger to help him," he said, giggling as he ran his small hand across the length of the gleaming vial. "In this time of times, I find it strangely ironic that I remain impervious to this fool's trickery, yet none of you do. You can thank this pompous hypocrite for that." Restlessly, he sighed. "Enough of this—I grow tired of this idiotic charade." Tapping a finger on the vial's glass casing, he threw them a cruel grin. Then, like a gruesome waxwork figure, his boyish facade melted away, transforming into its true form—Demora!

"It is truly laughable that this fool would have ever imagined that the very people he'd put his so-called faith in, would be the bringers of his own destruction." Afire from the fuel of her mounting hatred, *She* raised the Anfiora high above her head, and in one powerful motion, sent it smashing to the ground.

"No!" Preston yelled as the vial shattered into a thousand pieces. "You rotten glob of garbage, how could you do that?"

She gazed up at what remained of Damon's shimmering lifeforce, and waved a finger at him. "Do what? It's but useless mist—you would do well to place your concerns on matters much more pressing."

Lunging forward, Demora flung her arms at Preston, dragging him to her as Wil jumped to grab him. Instantly sprouting another limb, *She* hit Wil across the mid-section, launching him end over end.

In a blur, Samiel leapt toward Wil, and grabbed his hand. Sliding across the platform, they tried desperately to hold on, but their momentum sent them clean over the side. "Samiel!" Elex cried out as she crawled to the edge. Below her, he hung by one hand, gripping Wil with the other.

"Hold on!" she shouted, trying to reach him. "Grab my hand!"

A few feet away, Terrin and Paige stood frozen as they watched Demora morph into a monstrous winged beast, bringing down the arches like a house of cards. Piece by piece, the platform broke apart, falling into the flaming abyss below as its arches toppled against each other, crushing Elex beneath them. Screaming, Terrin pulled Paige to the stone walkway as Demora leapt into the air, carrying Preston up with her.

"Boy! You've missed the point all along," *She* roared, flying up toward the green mist that lingered above them. "Soon you'll understand—that I can assure you." Frantic, Preston dug his fingers into her scales as they were hit by a rolling wave of fire, sending them crashing back down onto the platform. Hitting the ground hard, Preston hung upside down in her grasp as *She* lay there stunned and shrouded in an emerald wildfire.

From across the cavern, the voice thundered down at them. "Demora! Once again, your hatred rains down on the earth—it must end now!"

Tossing Preston aside, *She* shifted into human form as the blaze that surrounded her turned indigo. "It is impossible—your wretched Anfiora is gone! That should have rid me of you!"

Above them, the mist whirled and tumbled, and washed down onto the pathway as it shaped itself into a sparkling vision of Damon Raydencrafft. "Sister, the ill-will you harbor continues to grow within you. Are you so blind that you fail to see it?"

"Fool! How dare you lecture me," Demora screamed. "No, *Brother,* it is you who are blind, for you fail to see that your precious world has become a den of murder and mayhem—a testament to your life's work gone to seed." Whipping around, *She* glared at Paige and Terrin with rage in her eyes, then reared back and launched a fiery mass of blue plasma that sprouted spikes as it rocketed toward them. Suddenly, the indigo nightmare ricocheted back at her, turning green as it impaled her. Engulfed in a raging inferno, *She* struggled to free herself as Damon's apparition loomed over her.

"Three hundred years—and you have learned nothing," Damon stormed as the aura surrounding him intensified. "To the last, you remain the same. You are lost."

Gazing up at him, *She* turned from grotesque to beautiful, her blazing copper hair flowing amid the flames of her emerald cage. "Brother—long ago, you loved me. Look at me—am I not as I once was?" *She* asked, beseeching him with radiant eyes of green and blue. "Your blood is mine, and mine yours—you cannot—you will not—hurt me again."

"You ask for compassion from one who cannot give it," he said somberly. "Our father received no such charity when you murdered him."

"*Father?* The vile swine was hardly that. He discarded me like trash," *She* shrieked scornfully. "Mark my words, Brother. The pitiful descendants of your ludicrous fellowship will submit or die as they beg at my feet!"

Damon glanced across the crumbling cavern as it quaked violently around them. "Sister, I fear there will be no end to the suffering you will cause. But even if what you say were true, you should still keep this in mind," he thundered, pointing to Paige and Preston. "They are the last in the line of the crescent order. I will not let you harm them." Breaking up against a gust of hot, steaming air, Damon's eerie pretense blew away as it covered the platform in a luminous firestorm. "The end draws near—you have failed. In your mindless desire to destroy me, you have unleashed a Pandora's Box that cannot be shut. Soon, you will pay for your transgressions, more than you will ever know." As his voice faded, Terrin backed away as she watched the raging tempest swirl down around Paige and Preston. Instantly, they both fell unconscious as she watched Demora thrash wildly within her smoldering prison.

"No! I was rid of you!" *She* screeched. "You were supposed to die! It is sacrilege—you've broken your own wretched law!" All around them, the mountain groaned as massive chucks of rock began to fall. One after another, the rocks miraculously missed the platform, until one came plunging at Demora.

Coldly, *She* watched it plummet towards her, staring at it in defiance. "Once again, this miserable planet spits upon me. Come—let me spew my last vengeful breath at you." CRASH! BOOM! Hitting full-force, the rock sent her tumbling along with a huge portion of the platform into the molten sea. Slowly, her fiery prison bobbed up and down as it sank into the flaming mire, and then, *She* vanished.

"Preston!" Terrin screamed as she shook him. "Preston, get up—please!"

He moaned as he opened his eyes and stared at the carnage around him. "Wha—what happened?" he sputtered.

Grabbing his hand, she pulled at him and pointed to the side of the platform. "It's Precept Dryden and Wil—you've got to help them—now! Hurry!"

Dazed, he pulled Terrin over to Paige, then slid to the edge as he dodged a barrage of falling debris. "Precept Dryden—Wil!" he yelled, reaching down. Gripping Samiel's hand, he pulled as hard as he could, trying to will himself the strength to pull them both up. "I can't do it," he shouted. "Come on—pull!" With one final rush of adrenaline, he pulled again, this time lifting them to safety. Quickly, they ran up to Elex and tried to clear away the rubble from her. "There's nothing we can do," Samiel snapped as lava spewed into the air around them, "I can't lift it!"

Without a word, Preston glared at the mountain of debris, when suddenly, his body erupted in a shower of flickering flames, turning the stone to dust. Sliding to Elex's side, Samiel's heart skipped a beat. "She's not breathing—we've got to get her out of here! Wil—Terrin—run to the other room!" Terrin grabbed Wil's hand and followed him as Samiel lifted Elex off the ground. Spinning around, he looked at Paige as she lay unconscious on the floor. "Preston! Pick her up and go!"

"But what about Mr. Jeffries?" he yelled, scooping Paige into his arms.

Samiel stopped at the walkway and waved Preston off. "I'll come back for him. Now go!"

Together, they ran across the narrow band of stone, and as they reached the halfway point, Paige came to and stared up at Preston. "What happened?" she asked as her eyes darted to the path. "Where am I?"

"Paige, I can't explain it right now—just hold on," he barked, increasing his pace as he focused on the exit. *Come on, Preston, keep running, it's just a little bit farther.*

KA_RRRANG! SMASH! A large chuck of the ceiling crashed down onto the pathway, reducing it to rubble. Hitting the brakes, Preston gawked at the gaping crevice. "Oh, that's great! What are we supposed to do now—*fly across?*" Gazing at the mountain in turmoil, Preston put Paige down and peered over the side, then dove towards the raging sea of fire.

"Preston!" Paige screamed as she grabbed Samiel. "Precept Dryden, what's happening?"

As if in answer, a gigantic raven, gleaming in turquoise blue, flew up behind them and carried them over the chasm. Dropping them at the entrance, the glowing bird hovered in front of them. "I've got to get Mr. Jeffries," Preston cawed as his wings kicked up a cloud of ash from the walkway. "Don't worry, I'll be back." Sharply turning away, he flew in the direction of the arched arena, evading falling rocks and flaming lava spouts as he soared across the void. In the distance, the stone platform came into view. Crumbling under the relentless quaking barrage, parts of it fell away as Preston swooped down and snatched Pete up in his claws. With lightning speed, he raced through the exit as the rock face came crashing down, sealing it shut.

Setting Pete down, he came to a standstill and shifted back to human form. "Precept Malineus?" he asked as she ran up to them, appearing no worse for wear. "But...uh, you—" Dumbfounded, he looked to Samiel for some sort of clue.

"Don't ask," Samiel said as he stared uneasily at Paige, "there's no explanation in the world that can explain away what I just saw." Suddenly, the hall shook from all sides as another tremor jolted the mountain. Frowning, Samiel glanced up at the ceiling as Pete sat up unsteadily and shook himself. "Pete—Elex, we've got to get moving, this mountain's coming down around our heads."

Retracing their steps, they bobbed and weaved through the maze of twisting tunnels, when at last, the greenery of the forest rushed at them. Breathless, they raced down the cliff-side trail, reaching the bottom minutes later.

"Once news of Demora's fate reaches her dark-seekers, there'll be no way to know what reprisals might await us," Samiel said as he gazed up at the mountain for the last time. "So, from now on, we've got to stay sharp and frosty, okay?" As they all nodded in agreement, Samiel gave them a warm smile, and then pressed forward through the dense tree line to start the first leg of the long journey home.

Chapter Thirty-One

The Way Home

"Cail's temple—*She* wrecked it," Preston whispered nervously. Staring through the thicket, he focused on the steps. "Precept Dryden, do you see anybody? It looks deserted."

"No—nothing, not a soul," Samiel said, sliding off his mount. "Pete, keep everyone back, I'm going to take a closer look." Cautiously, he climbed the steps, shaking his head as he studied the area around the entrance. "The stone's been liquefied—melted shut," he explained, jumping down the steps. "Demora wasn't exaggerating, your friend's sealed in tight as a drum." Waving everyone back, he let loose a blazing stream of red fire at the stone doors, and seconds later, they fell away in a molten waterworks. Extinguishing his hands, he absorbed the heat from the pools of liquid rock that remained, leaving lumps of misshapen stone in his wake.

Apprehensively, Preston inched up beside Samiel and peered in. "Cail? Where are you?" Scanning the ransacked antechamber, his gaze locked on yet another melted doorway.

With a scowl, Samiel moved across the room, then put his hand to it. Instantly, the surface lit up, covering the opening in indigo gel. "Preston, there's an earthborn energy field surrounding it," he said as Cail cried out from behind it. "Only an experienced wave would have a chance of getting through this barrier."

"But—we can't leave him in there. Cail, it's Preston—hold on, we'll get you out!" Closing his eyes, he placed his hands against the shield. With a blinding flash, the blue ooze turned to green, then vanished as the door fell away.

Bounding out of his prison like a boy shot from a cannon, the faerie ran straight at Preston, knocking him to the floor. "Come back, knew you would I did!" Cail said. "The wicked one, after you *She* is! Tried to harm me *She* did!"

"Cail, it's okay, *She's* gone," Preston said, staring grimly at what remained of the sprite's shrine. "I'm really sorry, we should've steered clear of you, then maybe *She* wouldn't have wrecked your home."

Cocking his head, Cail raised a brow at the notion, then danced circles around Preston. As he came to a stop, he wrinkled his nose at the gaping hole in the ceiling. "No matter it is—a shell of stone it has become. Too long in the forest dark I have been—too long. Go with you I will—yes?"

"Uh—well, we'll talk about that later, okay?" Preston said as Samiel glanced suspiciously at them. "Ummm, so—you want to camp with us tonight?" Giving Preston an enthusiastic yes, the faerie followed them outside and hopped down the steps.

"CAIL!" the girls shouted in chorus. "We missed you—are

you all right?"

(✝)

As Cail and the kids chattered back and forth, Pete watched them from a distance, then shook his head at Samiel and Elex. "You can't seriously be thinking of bringing him along, don't we have enough to worry about?" Samiel shrugged off his comment as Pete looked stubbornly at Elex. "Come on, if it wasn't for what the Brandymire girl did for you, we'd be discussing your funeral arrangements right now. So, if you don't mind, I'm keeping my eyes on the murderous little runt from now on."

Elex sighed as she squeezed Pete's hand and smiled, then headed off to help set up camp. Soon—adults, kids, and sprites alike were bantering on about all sorts of things as the day wound down to an end.

(✝)

"I never thought we'd make it back," Paige said as they rode down towards the conservatory. "But what now, I mean, they're probably going to expel us, aren't they?"

"Probably?" Preston asked incredulously. "Geez, we've broken almost every school rule there is and then some. And even worse, we've come back with squat—nothing. So, we might as well pack up and get out, before they kick us out."

Despite the gloom surrounding Preston, Cail grinned at him as if he hadn't a care in the world. "A shiny glass bottle the Anfiora needs not—other choices, other paths there are."

Maybe Cail's right—maybe we won't get expelled, Preston pondered as Manderlane Hall came into view. *Oh, who am I kidding? I've got to find Elise before it's too late to say goodbye.* Waiting for a good time to slip away, he trailed behind the group, then broke from the path and rode out of sight. At the girl's quarters, he snuck around the back, and climbed the fire escape to the third floor. Peering inside, he slipped in and hid in the corner. Carefully, he leaned to his left and stared down the hallway. A few girls were moving in and out of the hall when Aubree stepped out of the kitchen. "Aubree," he whispered as she went on with her business. "Psssst—Aubree, over here."

Spinning around, she squinted in his direction. "Preston?" she blurted out as he put a finger to his lips and waved her over to him.

"I don't have time to explain. Where's Elise?"

"She went to bed early," she said, frowning at him. "Ummm, she's been really down in the dumps lately."

"Can you get her?" he asked emphatically, "but I can't get caught in here, so don't tell her why, okay?"

Trying not to attract any attention, Aubree hurried down the hall and was soon heading back, pulling Elise behind her. As they turned the corner, Elise burst into tears. "Preston!" she cried, hugging him tight. "I thought I'd never see you again."

"Elise, I'm sorry, I wanted you to come with us, but I couldn't ask you to do that," he explained as she clung to him. "Besides, everything's gone wrong and it's all my fault."

"But you were just trying to do the right thing," she said tearfully. "That should count for something, shouldn't it?"

Preston dropped his head and spilled out a list of his offenses. "Sneaking out of school was bad—and stealing the food and the horses even worse. But refusing to follow Precept Dryden's orders—that was suicide," he said dejectedly. "And that's not even the worst part. Mr. Jeffries got hurt and Precept Malineus almost died. No, every single thing wound up being a complete car wreck."

Suddenly, Aubree's eyes widened as she ducked behind them.

"Elise, it's your sister, I think she saw us. Preston, you'd better go before—"

The rest of Aubree's warning went to the wayside as Meshel rounded the corner. "Before what?" she asked as her gaze came to rest on Preston. "Perfect—that figures. Precept Dryden's looking for you. He told me to take you straight to the chancellor's office if I found you."

Gasping in unison, Elise and Aubree gawked at Preston. "Preston, promise me you won't leave without saying goodbye," Elise pleaded as she turned pale. "Oh, I didn't mean that. It'll be okay, it has to be. Aubree, I'm right, aren't I?"

Aubree frowned at Elise as Meshel shook her head at her sister. "He's got to go now," she said sternly, pointing down the hall. "You both need to go to your quarters now. I'll be back after I drop him off."

Slowly, she escorted them through a gauntlet of awestruck girls, then pushed Elise and Aubree into their chamber. Throwing Elise one last awkward smile, Preston followed Meshel outside, and seconds later, they were barreling toward his impending doom. Once they reached Manderlane Hall, Preston lumbered up the steps and scowled as he stared at the hall's wooden doors. "It's not fair," he whispered. "I never did get them to work." *And I never will.*

On the ride up, Meshel eyed him as if trying to figure him out. As the lift opened, her expression turned serious. "Preston, I hope things work out for you. I'll never forget what you did for my sister, it said a lot about you." Giving him a quick hug, she stepped back into the elevator and smiled at him. "I can see why Elise really cares for you. Well, good luck."

Heavy-hearted, Preston walked through the empty lobby and into the hall of disappearing doors, hoping in desperation that the *trick* would somehow be in place. But as he turned the corner, he found the chancellor's office wide open, waiting for him. Stepping inside, he glanced around, then slowed to a crawl when he heard voices coming from within the hidden vault. "Wil? Terrin?" he asked, poking his head through the doorway. As he walked in, they both stepped out of the conference room, looking tired and brow-beaten.

"Are you guys okay?" he asked nervously. "Wil, where's Paige, and what did they say?" Before he could answer, Pete and Elex slipped up behind them, then Elex answered for him.

"Preston, this is very serious," Precept Malineus warned. "You do realize that, don't you?"

Preston shrunk as Pete patted him on the shoulder and grinned. "Well, at least the jury's still out. It appears that the powers that be are somewhat divided on what to do with you."

Pointing Preston in the right direction, Pete nudged Wil and Terrin toward the chancellor's office, stopping just shy of the door-way. "Preston, not that it matters at this point, but you've got our vote," he announced as Elex nodded in agreement. "Unfortunately, neither of our opinions amount to much."

With a sigh, Preston mulled over whether to turn tail and run, then took a deep breath and crept in. To his left, Mathias stood at the end of a large table. Natewick, Dean Dornquast, and Vice-Precept Lumenayre sat on either side of him. On the right, Samiel leaned ten-tatively against the wall as he listened to the vice-precept conclude her conversation with Paige. All the while, Cail happily hummed away in the drawing room next door.

"Preston, why don't you take a seat next to Paige," Dean Dornquast said, gazing at him through his rose colored spectacles. "All right—we've had a chance to talk to everyone involved in this *expedition* of yours, but we're still at a loss as to what to do about it. This is not to say that we don't understand your reasoning behind it, but your deliberate disregard for school policy has caused a hailstorm so large that we might not be able to quell the consequences of it. That aside, do you have anything you'd like to say first before we move on?"

Preston glanced uneasily at Paige, and then at Mathias, who quietly scribbled something on a notepad. "Sir, I know we broke the rules, but I don't think Wil and Terrin should get in trouble—they were just trying to help us" he explained. "I swear I never thought that things would turn out this way. We let her trick us again and everything got messed up because of it."

"Preston, I understand how it could look that way to you," Mathias said, drumming his fingers against the table, "but in this case, I believe that Damon knew all along that Demora would seek to destroy the Anfiora—and it was in that near certainty that he set his plan in motion."

Mathias pointed to the gleaming Laurelean Bloom hanging from Paige's neck and smiled. "Did you know the Anfiora and every known variety of bloom are tied together like electricity to a light bulb?" he asked as their faces went blank. "If the essence within the vial had actually been destroyed, then your stone would have gone dark permanently. But as you can see, it still glows."

"Hold on here, just what are ya suggesting?" Natewick asked. "That Damon's spirit is somehow floating in outer space or something ridiculous like that?"

Shaking his head, Mathias set his own bloom down in front of him, letting it fade. "No, it's more than that." With a wave of his hand, he guided the stone towards Preston, stopping it just short of him as the bloom lit up by itself. "Some sort of metaphysical event must have occurred at Ravyena," he said as the siblings gazed uneasily at each other. "I believe the Anfiora's energy has somehow fused itself to the aura surrounding you two."

"But I don't understand," Paige said, "I don't *feel* any different"

Natewick raised an eyebrow and frowned. "Mathias, I'm as baffled as she is. Even if this were true, and I'm not saying it is, what are ya proposing we do about it?"

"Do about it? There's nothing we can do at present. Fortunately, these two seem no worse for wear, so we'll circle the wagons and wait out the storm." Slapping the table, he rested his hands on the back of his chair and stared thoughtfully at Paige and Preston.

"All right, let's talk about this road trip of yours," he said as they sank in their seats. "Although you both used poor judgment by going out on your own, I still find it admirable that you felt strongly enough to take on such an undertaking." Sitting down across from them, he gave them both a stern look. "But I suggest that if there happens to be a next time, you might want to consider talking to us first."

Sheepishly, they both nodded as he smiled at them. "Good—okay then, after some serious thought, I've decided to issue all of you school citations for your efforts," he announced as their mouths dropped open. "From all accounts, each of you showed great courage and loyalty to those in your company. You stood by each other and remained strong—that in itself is a remarkable feat."

Getting up, he offered his hand to Samiel. "Thank you for bringing them home. I won't forget it," he said warmly, then shifted his gaze to the siblings. "Well, it's getting rather late and we could all use some rest. Samiel, would you mind escorting them to their chambers?"

"Oh, and regarding your friend in the next room," he added. "At present, he seems quite content to rummage through my collection. If he wants, we'll set something up for him on the grounds, perhaps a bungalow of some sort. But for the time being, he can stay with me—to be honest, he's starting to grow on me."

Smirking, Preston closed an eye as he slipped his baseball cap on. "Yeah, it really doesn't take long, does it?"

"School citations? After all that's happened? Mathias, you certainly have a knack for stirring the pot at the worst of times," Dean Dornquast pointed out. "Surely, you have to know that Vice-Chancellor Cabriel's not going to be happy about this."

Raising a brow, Mathias sighed as he checked on Cail, who continued to tinker with the various knickknacks around him. "You let me worry about the vice-chancellor, but I need you and Valerian to keep a close watch on the Brandymire children. There are far too many forces trying to influence future events to leave things to chance alone."

"But aren't we forgetting about Demora?" the vice-precept said anxiously. "How can we be certain that *She* perished? And what of her dark-followers, I can only begin to imagine the havoc they might wreak upon us."

Shaking his head, he gave her a sobering look. "You're right, there's no way to be sure, but it's clear that we must remain on constant guard. For now, we'll keep our distance and let the wolves come to us. That way, we can see them as they make their approach from afar—"

Chapter Thirty-Two

The Long Goodbye

Finals came and went without a hitch, signaling the beginning of what Paige hoped would be a blissfully uneventful summer. All over campus, the atmosphere was electric as everyone got ready to head home for two and a half glorious months.

Paige and Terrin stepped outside the girl's quarters and gazed out over the sea of students. "Wow, I can't believe we actually made it all the way to the end," Terrin said excitedly. "Can you pinch me? Because I think I'm dreaming."

In fun, Paige reached out and tried to do just that as Terrin hopped down a couple of steps and scowled at her. "Hey, I didn't mean for you to *actually* do it," she said, then changed the subject. "Ummm, didn't Aubree say they'd be right down? What's taking them so long?"

Paige peered inside as Aubree and Elise came bounding down the stairs and out the door. "What time did we sign up for?" Aubree asked as Elise fidgeted beside her. "I hope we're not late."

Squinting at the clock tower, Paige glanced at the departure schedule. "We're fine," she said, looking toward Manderlane Hall. "But we'd better go—Preston said they'd meet us at the hall."

Quickly, they weaved their way through the torrent of chattering students, reaching the hall in minutes. "Where are they?" Paige shouted over the noise of the crowd. "They were supposed to be here by now."

Squeezing through the throng of kids, they spilled out onto the bridge, and searched the crowd on their tiptoes. "There they are—with Mr. Beadle and Chancellor Manderlane," Terrin said, tugging on Paige's jacket as Natewick waved in their direction, "and Cail too."

"There ya are missy. We've been waiting to see ya off," Natewick said cheerfully. "Oh, and I see ya and Terrin are wearing your shiny new citation pins—very impressive."

Blushing, Paige smiled at him and gave him a hug. "I'm really going to miss you," she said, clutching her Laurelean Bloom, "but this will remind me of you."

"Missy, for me, ya'll be equally hard to forget," he said, beaming from ear to ear, "but in a couple of months, ya'll be back, and then we'll have plenty to talk about for sure."

"All right, I hate to cut things short, but it looks like your ride's here," Mathias said, grinning at them. "We'll see you all again in the fall, have a great summer." He shook each of their hands before sending them on their way, pausing at Preston and Paige. "You take care of each other, okay?" he said, handing them each a small emerald pouch. "I thought you might enjoy these, they belonged to me and my sister—you can open them a little later." Paige ran up and hugged him as the others headed to the elevator. "Well, young lady, you better hurry. Silas is definitely a man who keeps a tight schedule. Have a safe trip and remember to steer your brother away from trouble."

Halfheartedly, they climbed into the glass lift as Cail ran up to them. "Wish you well do I," he said with a sad smile. "Be here when you come back I will." Waving goodbye, they made their slow ascent up to the Crittendome Skydock as Preston watched the conservatory grow smaller and smaller.

"Preston, promise me you'll call as much as you can," Elise said quietly. "You know, we really don't live that far from each other. Maybe we can talk our parents into letting us meet half way."

With a crooked smirk, he gazed into her golden eyes. "Elise, after all we've been through, they'll have to lock me up and throw away the key to keep me from seeing you this summer."

Slipping his cap off, he placed it over her head, and admired its new home. "This has given me a whole lot of luck," he said as she pulled it down just above her eyes, "it'll bring you the same. Besides, it looks way better on you."

Abruptly, the elevator rumbled to a stop and as they all filed out onto the dock, Silas poked his head out from behind the control booth. "Well, a big hello ta one and all of ya. Ya certainly picked a splendid day ta go on a summer holiday. Ah, summer, I've had a lot of rip roaring ones in my day, but that's another story," he said, twisting the ends of his moustache. "I'm sad ta say that I won't be taking ya across myself. Gotta heavy schedule ta keep as ya know, but I surely hope ya'll have a beauty of a summer."

After a wave from Silas, they piled into a waiting skycar, and were sent on their way. At a leisurely pace, the glass gondola floated over the campus, and then, as if waking from a dream, Raydencrafft was gone.

"Geez, that didn't take long at all. We're almost on the other side," Jim announced as they stared at the approaching skydock.

Seconds later, their skycar floated into the dock and stopped, and like kids loose in an amusement park, they ran from one ride into the next. "Yes! This is where the fun really begins," Preston exclaimed, "because it's time for roaring railcars! Hey, Elise and I got dibs on the last car." Helping Elise climb in, he jumped in after her and watched as the girls headed to the front. "Oh, no way—Paige, you're not chickening out again, are you? Okay, it's your choice, but I'm telling you, you're missing out."

RUMBLE! CLUNK! The railcars jerked forward as the burly trainman bellowed, "Next stop—the railcar dock." Traveling down through the mountain at the speed of a runaway mining car, they barreled through the tunnels as Jim bellowed out his best ghost sounds all the way.

"Uh, well, we're here," Preston said as they rolled into the dock. "This is it, I guess." Frowning, Elise looked absolutely gloomy in the emerald light as Aaron and Wil ambled up to them.

"Is it me or was the ride a lot shorter this time around?" Aaron asked, gazing around the dock. "Hey, hold on, didn't they say our stuff would be waiting for us?"

With a big grin, Wil pointed to the exit. "Thayne said we'd be picking them up at the bottom of the hill," he informed him as another thought popped into his head. "Hey, before I forget, did everyone get each other's number?" Collectively, they shook their heads, then entered the passage leading to the clearing outside. Working their way through the maze, they slipped in and out of the shadows until the sun peeked in from the railcar entrance.

"Mom! Dad!" Paige and Preston yelled as they all scrambled out into the sunlight. Wide-eyed, Paige fidgeted as Preston tried to split his attention between them and Elise.

"Mom—look! Preston and I got special awards from the chancellor," she said, pointing to her jacket collar. "Oh, and you're never going to guess what happened." As Paige rattled off the highlights, Preston peered at Elise from afar, then started to squirm as she walked his direction with her family.

"Mom—Dad—this is the boy Meshel told you about," Elise said, throwing him a coy look. "Preston, these are my parents and this is my little sister April."

Elise's mother gave him a bright smile as her father patted him on the back. "Son, it's a pleasure," he said. "I can't thank you enough for what you did for our daughter. If there's anything we can ever do for you, all you have to do is ask."

"Thank you, sir," Preston said, watching his parent's eyes widen. "I'd do it again in a heartbeat." Quickly, he introduced Paige and his puzzled parents to them and soon they were all chatting back and forth about everything from school to the drive home.

As things wound to a close, Wil ran up to them, beaming from ear to ear. "Well, we're leaving. Elise, you take it easy. And Preston, don't forget to call me." Running towards his parent's car, he turned and pointed a finger at Preston. "Oh, yeah, and try to stay out of trouble—because I won't be around to bail you out."

Laughing, Preston smirked at him as he waved goodbye. "Hey, what could go wrong? Just think about it, we were almost expelled and now they're calling us heroes. Summer's going to be a breeze compared to that."

M. ALAN YATES WAS BORN IN A SLEEPY TOWN OVERLOOKING THE CHAOTIC STREETS OF THE BIG CITY. GROWING UP ON A STEADY DIET OF COMIC BOOKS AND TV HEROES, HE DREAMT OF ONE DAY CREATING A WORLD OF HIS OWN...A PLACE TO ESCAPE FROM THE HARSH GLARE OF THE WORLD.

THE AUTHOR'S WEB SITE IS WWW.RAYDENCRAFFT.COM.

COVER ART BY M. ALAN YATES

www.ingramcontent.com/pod-product-compliance
Lightning Source LLC
Chambersburg PA
CBHW050732180626
46814CB00002B/719